Mrs Funnybones Returns

Mrs Funnybones Returns

Twinkle Khanna

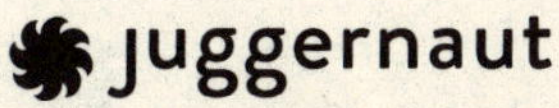
juggernaut

JUGGERNAUT BOOKS
C-I-128, First Floor, Sangam Vihar, Near Holi Chowk,
New Delhi 110080, India

First published by Juggernaut Books 2025

10 9 8 7 6 5 4 3 2 1

P-ISBN: 9789353456207
E-ISBN: 9789353453626

Typeset in Adobe Caslon Pro by R. Ajith Kumar, Noida

Printed at Thomson Press India Ltd

CONTENTS

1

FOR GOD'S SAKE, CAN YOU FIND MY PHONE?

7 a.m.: The phone rings and an unknown voice says, 'Hullo, who you speaking?' I immediately reply, 'I am Beena Thomas, nurse at Holy Family Hospital,' and the phone is promptly disconnected.

No, I haven't developed a multiple personality disorder. This is simply to dissuade random people, who spend the same amount of time excavating my phone number as the police spend digging up skeletons in Penn, from calling me to say, 'Sister, what your sweet name, Tinkle na?'

8.15 a.m.: Instead of getting ready for our trek, I call my sister to complain, 'It's so hot that even my ovaries are popping out boiled eggs, I don't know why we have to go on this sweaty expedition.'

My sister replies, 'If your ovaries are popping out scrambled, fried, boiled, actually any sort of eggs at all at this age, then it's a miracle. Stop being lazy and get on with it.'

Knowing she is right, I grudgingly put on my sneakers.

10.30 a.m.: We bundle up the children, load the car with an icebox filled with sandwiches and other goodies, and head off for our much-awaited picnic in the wilderness. All the phones are on silent according to our picnic pact so that we talk to each other and not to random voices floating on radio signals.

The prodigal son, sprawled over the backseat, is trying to watch a show on his iPad and I have to remind him that it's our 'No-Gadget Day'. He reluctantly tucks it away, and perhaps in retaliation, starts tugging at his seatbelt, saying,

'I am wearing my seatbelt only because you are driving.'

I reply, 'That's terribly sexist, you know!'

And pat comes his answer, 'It would be sexist if I said all women are bad drivers. Here, I am referring to just you.'

In the midst of arguing with the man of the house about why left is right and right is wrong and not just when you are driving, I glance at the rearview mirror and notice that my younger one is busy texting. I reprimand her and Miss Smarty Pants wails, 'But I want to talk to Anya.'

Feeling more like a prison warden than a participant in this family outing, I reply, 'And I want to talk to Brad Pitt, but we can't always get what we want, so put that phone away.'

11.20 a.m.: The four of us are standing below a deserted hillock. The sun is already beating down on us, and that, mixed with four meagre hours of sleep and two drinks at a wedding the night before, seems to make this pimple-sized hill as daunting as climbing Mount Everest. Luckily, I have two Punjabi Sherpas of my own, and I hand them the icebox, strengthen my resolve, grab the younger one and off we go.

11.45 a.m.: 'I have to go to bathroom,' chimes Miss Smarty Pants, and though I give her a pick of various bushes, all lined up in the toilet with the highest blue ceiling made by God Himself, she is not satisfied. 'What if something bites my bottom?' she asks. Finally, just as she agrees to squat, she repeats her favourite questions, 'Mama, you always say that God is everywhere. So is God in the sky? Is He in the bush? Is He in the grass?' And when I nod yes, she asks, 'So if God is everywhere then when I am peeing, am I doing it on Him?'

1 p.m.: We find a spot beneath a lush banyan tree, and I open the icebox and hand my younger one a sandwich. She immediately pulls it apart and starts discarding the salad. I try coaxing her into eating the tomatoes slices with a joke, 'Do you know what the tomato fleeing the Heinz

factory told his slow-poke brother? "Catch up or ketchup!"' The prodigal son immediately chimes in, 'Mom, please never make these jokes in public, people will throw so many eggs and tomatoes that you can make masala omelettes for a month.'

'Let them,' I say, 'I am happy to save on my grocery bills. I have only one caveat: I want to know the religion of everyone throwing these ingredients my way. If any of them are Buddhist, I will not accept any deliveries from them.'

'Why? What have the poor Buddhists done to you now ?' the man of the house asks.

'I am just trying to be inclusive. If people can take umbrage against so many religions, then why make the Buddhists feel left out? Someone should be offended by them as well, right?'

He looks at me perplexed and I continue. 'Haven't you heard? Some dude ordered food on Zomato and then wanted to cancel his order because the delivery man was a "non-Hindu".'

I stop Miss Smarty Pants from surreptitiously pushing bits of cucumber under the picnic blanket, and say, 'I don't know why people make religion so complicated. If you ask me, I think the core of all spiritual beliefs is like the recipe of a basic sponge cake. The ingredients are the same – charity, peace, tolerance. The rest is just different sorts of icing – pick one that suits you best, butter cream or chocolate glaze. It's the same as choosing to eat a certain animal or not. Fasting once a week through the year, or one month at a time. Talking to God on Fridays or Sundays. I think even this one God versus multiple gods is not very different from the concept of an entire cake versus pastries. If you ask me, religious conflicts are just caused by people licking the icing rather than digging into the cake.'

My younger one interrupts, 'Where have you packed cake? I want some cake.'

The prodigal son laughs, 'There is no real cake, dummy, this is just one of Mom's weird analogies, get used to it!'

I sigh, 'You know, all this wisdom that I waste on you people, I should just save it and one day start a satsang of my own. You guys watch, while the world is going completely bananas, Baba

Twinkdev's Art of Cake Engineering will be the akela one worth following!' My words are drowned out by my younger one now chanting, 'Cake! Cake! Cake!'

2.30 p.m.: Rocks have been climbed and minor cliffs have been scaled when we finally return to our faded blanket on the dusty ground and lie down flat on our backs in the shade. The sun dapples a moving print of shadowy leaves on our arms and stomachs as we look up at the partly cloudy sky through the tangle of branches. There is silence, a still silence where you can hear tiny insects in a nearby shrub, the sound of waves on the other side of the cliff, and breaths long held now slowly exhaled.

3.40 p.m.: It's time to leave and a phone is pulled out for the first time in hours. Despite my protests, we are going back by another route that involves catching a ferry and organising a car to wait on the other side.

4.15 p.m.: It's chaos. The ferry is packed with people, each with a phone in hand and all wanting selfies with the man of the house.

4.30 p.m.: We scramble into the car, and while looking for a packet of chewing gum, I realise that my phone is missing from my back pocket. Grabbing the man of the house's phone, I try dialling my number, and though I can hear it ringing at the other end, there is no sound in the car. My older one postulates that it must have fallen near the dock and then has another brainwave. He pulls out his iPad and says, 'I can trace your phone.' And sure enough, there on the iPad screen is my phone. It is about two kilometres away in the opposite direction. I beg the man of the house to turn and drive towards my phone. He grumbles under his breath but gives in.

4.35 p.m.: We are racing towards the blip on the iPad when the prodigal son says, 'Mom! I think someone has picked up your phone because it is now coming towards us.' We try calling but the other person doesn't pick up.

The prodigal son says, 'Park on the side, Dad, and get down! That man is somewhere here, I can see it on the iPad, he is almost next to us!'

The man of the house refuses and I snap, 'Can't you do this much for me! Shah Jahan can build Taj Mahal for his beloved, and you can't even step out of this car!'

The prodigal son says, 'Dad, he is getting away, let's chase him!'

And off we go, chasing the moving blip that represents my phone.

4.45 p.m.: The man must be on a bike because he is moving fast and we finally give up. The prodigal son says, 'Mom, I can erase your phone and all your data from our iPad, then he can't use it. Should I?' And feeling like Putin ordering a missile strike, I say, 'Yes, destroy it!'

5.15 p.m.: Our No-Gadget Day has gone down the drain. I am now frantically using the man of the house's phone, trying to get a new one for myself because obviously I may die if a day passes without odd people calling me, spouting nonsense like, 'Bhabhi ji, I want your good friendship!'

5.40 p.m.: We are home, and as I get out of the car in a foul mood, I hear a clink. There on the floor is my cracked, erased and now deceased phone. It was in the car all along with the ringer turned off. There was no mysterious man with a moustache or a mole on a motorbike as we had imagined. We had been chasing our own tails and a signal lag. All this rubbish technology did was prevent us from checking the car thoroughly.

7.20 p.m.: Disgruntled and, I hate to admit it, bored, without my phone, I decide to visit my mother. Chomping on a bowl of makhanas, I start telling her about my disastrous day. 'Mom, don't you think it's become an epidemic?'

'What?' she says, 'Is Covid back?'

'No, I am talking about this phone menace. Everywhere you look, people have their heads bent over their tiny screens.'

My mother interrupts me to tell me that she has found a vase that she thinks I should buy and starts showing me the pictures on Instagram.

I protest, 'This is exactly my point. Again there is a screen in the middle, turning a simple one-on-one conversation into yet another threesome.'

'Another threesome! Beta, I hope you are not turning experimental at this age.'

'No, I didn't mean it literally, Mom. God, what is the point of talking to you! Sometimes I wish Hema Malini was my mother instead, at least I would get a Kent water purifier free.'

9 p.m.: Over dinner, I tell the man of the house about my exchange with my mother. 'I can never talk to Mom without her showing me some antiques on her phone,' I say. 'These gadgets have really taken over our lives. I mean, go to any restaurant and you will see couples sitting together at a table but looking at their respective screens. We take selfies together before we even look into each other's eyes. We call our friends less, because to press "like" on Instagram is not as complicated.

These machines were meant to free us. But now we are enslaved by the very freedom we pursued, as heads bent and eyes lowered, we look solely at our masters as we tap away.'

The man of the house sighs, 'Arre, why can't you be like the phone in my pocket right now?'

I say, 'What? Stuck to your thigh?'

He replies, 'No! Just on silent mode.'

Standing beside every great man, there is often a woman constantly telling him what he is doing wrong. And she is usually right.

2

MOTHERHOOD, KAL AND AAJ

As a child in the '70s, I recall my mother's duties being clearly defined. The most important was ensuring we finished the two rotis on our plate. In my sister's case, this was an arduous task as Mom had to keep poking her younger child's cheek where lumps of masticated wheat were deposited like they were gathering compound interest. Others revolved around completing our homework and the mandatory braiding of hair. Sometimes not satisfied with two pigtails, these plaits were twisted back to the sides of our heads and fastened with a ribbon, so we looked more like goats with flapping ears than little girls.

Aside from these daily rituals, we were left to our own devices. This meant we had ample time to chase chickens in a nearby dump or run down the lane to Gopal's shop for sweets on credit. We even had a 'setting' with the juicewala on the beach. Along with selling sugarcane juice and ice-cold colas, he saved us all the bottle caps of Gold Spot.

During that time, the most significant event in our lives was the announcement of Gold Spot's famous contest, where bottle caps with *Jungle Book* characters could be exchanged for a prize.

Like the other mothers of that time, my mother was not particularly bothered by our dubious social activities as long as we didn't argue and performed a decent namaste in front of guests.

When I compare what motherhood meant when I was a child to what I have to undertake as a modern mother, it is terrifying.

My initiation into motherhood began in 2002 when my son was born. This was the time when my husband told a visitor that I was unavailable because I was 'milking' and immediately sealed my transformation from a hot chick to a cow. It was also a period when an entire generation of mothers would show newborns Baby Einstein videos to stimulate their brains. It didn't occur to anyone that not only did Einstein's mother not play any videos for her son, but as evident in her letters, she was primarily preoccupied with his appearance instead of his intellect. In her memoirs, Einstein's wife states that just before the genius was about to receive the Nobel Prize, his mother rushed towards him with a comb and said, 'There is nothing I or anyone, with the exception perhaps of God, can do about your great big darling deformed head. But there is something we can do about your hair.'

Hair, as we have already established, has always been a large part of mothering. Though the mothers of the '70s and '80s often had to moonlight as hairdressers, modern mothers, besides having hairdressing skills, are meant to be therapists, event planners, stylists, educators, motivational coaches and nutritionists rolled into one.

We must also preferably hold down jobs with one hand and our children with the other. We must breastfeed but not have droopy breasts. We must shovel the right combination of nutrients down their throats and avoid eating their leftovers to reacquire the waistlines we once had before these creatures turned our wombs into their personal campervans. We must ensure they are entertained, mingle with the right peers and praise their lopsided drawings like we are courtiers bowing to the emperor with no clothes. All this should be accomplished by a method called 'gentle parenting', unlike our mothers who ordered us around like army colonels.

In pursuit of this parenting style, my bedtime routine with my younger one often stretches endlessly as I combat questions like why it matters that you brush your teeth every night, even if those teeth will fall off soon enough. To get her off the iPad, I need to deploy statistics about the surge of myopia in children.

In the list of roles a mother needs to play today, I omitted mentioning the largest one – becoming a screen-time monitor. Looking at all these children with their heads bent over flickering screens, I can't help feeling a certain nostalgia for a time when our imaginations were our greatest tools.

We strained bougainvillea flowers to create tinted water that we applied on cheeks and T-shirts. We turned rainwater-filled potholes into our own French Riviera, where we would set sail paper boats made of newspapers and marksheets. Today, we are likely to stop our children from playing in muddy puddles and run behind them with sanitiser to attack germs.

While the modern mother does ensure her children are safer than previous generations, I wonder if we are wrapping them in so many layers of bubble wrap that they cannot experience the real world except as a hazy blur. Are we doing them a disservice by raising them in a homogenised, sanitised world where they play the same games online and have the same extracurricular activities? Is that why the current generation, with their similar mannerisms, clothes and interests, all seem like clones of each other?

In the playground of modern motherhood, the seesaw between security and liberty has a prominent place. Too much freedom, and you will be seen as uninvolved. Too little, and you are stifling them. This journey through the landscape of motherhood, kal and aaj, remains unchanged, along with the requisite blame and guilt.

Perhaps this Mother's Day, instead of flowers or candy, I will reserve my present for the future. One day I would like to receive the gift I finally gave my mother. I erased her saintly pedestal of motherhood because pedestals are narrow by nature, and it only takes one twirl to fall.

In my forties, I gave my mother the gift of acceptance. I let her know that I didn't blame her for any inadvertent slip-ups. After having my children, I understood that our job as mothers is not to give our children perfect childhoods but to love them dearly and do our best within our inherent limitations.

If I am honest, I haven't given her complete absolution yet. I am holding a bit back until she lets go of a peculiar habit. There has never been a significant event in my life where my mother, instead of being excited about my achievements, has not started fretting about my hair and, with a worried frown, reached out to put stray strands in place. On this front, I can safely state that Einstein and I have something in common: our mothers' obsession with our hair.

There was more that I had to say about motherhood, but by the time I reached the penultimate paragraph, my younger one began asking for her screen password. After negotiating with her, I couldn't quite remember the points for my grand finale.

Clearly, in some cases, motherhood is a journey where someone constantly pulls the emergency chain and halts your train of thought.

3

MARRIED NOT BRANDED

8 a.m.: Sipping on my first cup of coffee, I tell my sister, 'You know I was so upset that I was sick last week, but now I look at it as a blessing. I didn't have to go to any of those Mehta wedding functions, and I saw what they were all wearing on Instagram anyway. Loose motions is not a bad thing, by the way, it's not just the perfect excuse to stay at home but also I have lost a few pounds.'

She is getting grouchy in her perimenopause years because she snaps at me, 'Every week you give me an update of how much weight you have lost and gained! It's not the rupee against the dollar that anyone has such deep interest in your 0.5 shifting parameters.'

11.45 a.m.: After three hours of taking a guillotine to my new manuscript, I am saved by the bell. My newly single and more than willing to mingle friend walks in with two Frappuccinos and a bad mood. 'This dating thing is frightening. In this day and age, you can't send a single message without worrying that the whole world will see it! Bas, people now just take screenshots and out it goes,' she says.

I reply, 'Well, if it's really something explicit, then isn't it better to just call instead of sexting?'

'People can also record conversations you know,' she adds.

I thank my lucky stars that my dating days seem to be behind me, have a sip of my Frappuccino and say, 'All right, I have an idea, next time just call the guy, pant on the phone and hang up. If he ever records and plays it for anyone, you can always say you were doing aerobics.'

'You are really so uncool. No one does aerobics anymore! Oof, I really hate all this technology, it was so much simpler in the '90s.'

I reply, 'Arre be grateful! Weren't you able to be part of the Ambani wedding? Thanks to social media, we are all attending weddings, some that we are not invited to, without even having to shell out for a halfway decent gift.'

3 p.m.: We pop over to my mother's and find her head buried in *Many Lives, Many Masters*. I call out to her and she replies with, 'Hi Endometriosis!'

Accustomed to her endless pet names like Diamond, Lady Diana and even Alfred, I am still taken aback at being affectionally called by a term describing a menstrual ailment.

When I protest, she cheerfully explains, 'What's wrong with it? In this birth you are my child, in another you can be a cyst, and in a third you could just have been endometriosis.'

And off she goes into the kitchen, leaving the twin pillars of Hinduism and karma shaking at their knees along with me.

3.15 p.m.: We are now being forced to try the khandvi that she has bought in anticipation of my nana's overbearing cousin Champa Ben's monthly visit. When I protest that I don't like this particular dish – it's slimy and makes me feel like there is a large yellow worm sliding along my tongue – she informs me that I have always had terrible taste and brings up the time when I rejected her advice and refused to wear an embroidered shawl as a cape. My defence, that I was going for a fashion show and it was not a shawl but a blanket she had bought in Manali, doesn't seem to hold any weight in her court of maternal justice.

6 p.m.: Jamnagar making news on the global stage because of the Ambani celebrations had made Champa Ben's heart swell like a pea-stuffed kachori. On the extended family WhatsApp group, not only had she posted pictures of the three Khans performing together on stage but also a video of Mark Zuckerberg gushing over Anant Ambani's watch with a comment, 'Amara

Facebookwallah has also never seen such tope-class items.'

After dissecting the Ambani wedding once again at great length, Champa Ben decides to focus on us. 'Kamaal che, even these modern girls like Radhika are changing their last name but you two sisters have still not changed.'

I laugh. 'If I had to change my name, Champa Ben, trust me I would change my first name and not my last. We are married, not branded, you know?'

'Huh?' Is Champa Ben's eloquent response.

'Branded like a cow or, for that matter, taken over by a company. It's not like Rinke and I are two small businesses that have been bought by Godrej so now we have to change our brand name to theirs na?' I reply.

After fifteen years of being married, I wonder why people still ask me this question. Isn't it odder that only one partner has to redesign their identity, wipe out their past, while the other one goes through the transition unchanged?

My mother has a sip of her tea. 'Khanna sisters now and forever, these two keep saying. Pagal sisters would be more apt.'

Trying to save us from another of Mother Dearest's lengthy lectures, my sister changes the subject quickly. 'Did you catch all those Meghan Markle interviews? At first it felt like a fairytale wedding, but after seeing all that royal family drama, I don't think she has had it easy.'

'I guess it's not easy being married at all,' I say. 'We give up homes, jobs, names and bend over backwards to please, till a few years later we find ourselves lying horizontal on our backs, hoping no one walks all over us.'

I think about my younger one and wonder if, after she is married, she will change, add on or stick to her already hyphenated last names. How odd that these questions won't even arise regarding the prodigal son. The same way that we have always been worried about our girls and not as much about our boys. Keeping the room door open when the tuition sir comes over; ensuring that the school bus has a female chaperone;

making sure that as little girls, they were not alone with even men from the extended family; and, along with all this, trying to strike a delicate balance between teaching them to be on guard and yet not be frightened of the world.

My sister interrupts my meandering thoughts. 'You are talking about last names, but what about all the taam-jhaam we will have to do? The bar is now set very high after the Ambani events. If no one else, then at least Champa Ben will judge us,' she laughs.

I reply, 'Well, I can't dance like Nita Bhabhi. The last time I tried dancing to "Tamma Loge" during the pandemic, I think even God didn't want to see my uncoordinated footwork because I immediately fell down and fractured my leg. My husband can barely stay awake after 10 p.m., and we both get anxious about hosting dinner parties for over twenty people.' I pause for breath. 'If my children really want me to be happy, then the best thing they can do is just elope.'

Champa Ben looks at me disapprovingly and then says, 'Bou, pat pat na kar, here, eat something,' passing the plate of khandvi to me. 'You girls have to learn to bend a little, Beta. Young people have no tolerance.'

'Champa Ben, tolerance is what a bacteria develops against an antibiotic, where both remain unchanged, indifferent to each other's presence,' I say. 'I think sometimes it's better to chafe against each other and like a particle in an oyster, you may just grow a pearl. Or perhaps help each other, like the birds that hang out with zebras and eat ticks off their backs. But most importantly, you should support each other, have a great partnership like ...'

And as I am racking my brains for the perfect pair, Champa Ben pops in again with, 'Like apno Modi and Amit Bhai.'

That wasn't exactly the pair I had in mind but I guess it's as good an example as any.

Humour is like
deodorant.
You can live without it.
But if you use it,
you make life easier
for everyone around you,
including yourself.

4

HOW TO SAY NO TO MAMI JI'S HALWA

'Are you free tomorrow at 3? I need a favour,' asked an old acquaintance with an exotic mix of British and Goan accents, the absence of the letter h in the three as obvious as a missing front tooth. I looked up at him, the sun making me squint, causing the reappearance of pesky floaters in my left eye and creating a halo around his curly mop.

'What do you need?'

'My girlfriend is having an exhibition at the restaurant. Can you inaugurate it and take some pictures with her for the paper?'

In the decade I have had a home in Goa, I have tried to match my routine to that of a sloth. Each day consists of riding my yellow scooter to the beach, reading books in a hammock and watching the bats quench their thirst in our pool. Cutting a ribbon while grinning for photographers sounded awful. After an awkward pause, I said, 'Uh ... okay, totally no, of course, yes.' A sentence that made no sense but for the nodding of my head, which indicated an affirmative response.

When he moved on to greet other customers, my friend sitting at the table, with a mouth full of buttered poi, grumbled, 'I can't believe you said yes to that.'

'I didn't want to,' I protested, 'Forget proper clothes, I don't even have a car here! Do you know how stupid I am going to look arriving for this inauguration in front of the press on my bloody scooter! Now I have already agreed, so let's just finish it off.'

I prepared for this momentous event by finding a dingy salon, getting a terrible blow-dry and buying a new dress. When we arrived at the restaurant, it was deserted. Well, aside from a few blue streamers strung across the ceiling and the owner with a white bandage on his head. We discovered his girlfriend had broken up with him. He had then gone on a drinking binge, fallen down a flight of stairs and drunk some more to numb the pain. He suddenly rose from his mumbling stupor and decided that we must all have a good time. My friend was pulled to dance and unceremoniously twirled about. ABBA's 'Dancing Queen' was remixed with a cry of pain, as she hit her shoulder against a pole. After that he climbed onto the table. Just when I thought there was another bout of stumbling samba on the cards, he passed out, his legs hanging off one end of the table.

We scrambled out with our injured bits, her shoulder and my pride. On the way back, she berated me, 'I told you we should not go, why the hell did you agree to this idiotic thing?'

And the truth came out. 'I guess, I just didn't know how to say no.'

I am not the only one who has been in a situation where there is a 'No' with an exclamation mark looming inside my head, but a tepid 'Yes' pops out of the mouth instead.

This daft exchange happens for myriad reasons. From worrying about acceptance and wanting to avoid criticism, to fear of the consequences linked to refusal.

Also, coming across as an agreeable, likeable person is a hardwired evolutionary instinct.

In the Palaeolithic Age, if members of the tribe did not like you, then during scarcity, guess who would go without food, or perhaps even find themselves tied to a log and roasting over a fire? Clearly not Ms Popular with a wide smile and ability to nod enthusiastically. Though we no longer depend as strongly on approval in order to survive, we still find it difficult to turn people down.

No is a fortress that can shield us from wasting time and energy.

Yes is the drawbridge that lets others inside our domain. If the drawbridge is lowered repeatedly, then we end up overwhelmed. On the other hand, if always sealed, then we end up missing out. Balance, as boring as it sounds when prescribed as part of a nutrition plan, is the key.

In the last month itself I have been asked to 'Write a foreword for my book', 'Have another helping, Mami ji made the halwa herself', 'Ask your husband to make a video wishing my cousin's son happy birthday!', 'Try some sheesha, don't be a bore', 'Can you help rewrite my daughter's college essay?', 'Since you loved Mami ji's halwa, have some laddoos, she has made them only for you!'

If I agreed to all these requests, I would be an obese, stressed-out wreck with eventual impaired lung function. In the end, I did cave in to some because I didn't want to hurt the other person's feelings. I then set out to discover how to say no gracefully. Here is what I found.

The Mannat Policy: In a podcast by Tim Ferris, he talks about well-crafted rejection letters that people sent him for his book. He says these letters are successful at their task because they don't make the recipient feel that it's personal. Each one explained their predicament and then added different iterations of 'Turning down things as a blanket policy'.

When I asked a cousin what she does to get out of situations, she gave me the Indian version of a blanket policy, 'Oh, I just say I can't do it because I have taken a mannat.'

The Timely Pause: *Tweak*'s editor suggested the buying-more-time strategy. Stalling is also advocated by psychotherapist Julie Bjelland. 'Let me think about it and get back to you' gives you enough time to evaluate the request and come up with the right words to reject it.

The Switcheroo Method: Providing an alternative is my favourite because, along with appeasing others, it makes me feel less guilty as well. 'Come over for a drink and don't make any more excuses,' was a friend's slightly annoyed request. Considering my New Year's Eve hangover had left me feeling like I would have suffered less if

I'd have contracted a moderate case of Covid-19, I shot back with, 'I would love to, but I'm not drinking these days, let's go for a walk instead!' and our equation veered back from being as frozen as her recently renovated forehead.

The Speechless Spell: This relies on shock value. The other person is so taken aback that they can't protest. 'I can't, yaar, I am feeling guilty, I haven't spent enough time with my cat,' is a frequent excuse used by a co-worker. Then it's things like, 'My astrologer says I have to avoid going out on Fridays.'

One of the best excuses I have heard came from a well-known actress who told a common friend, 'I can't come darling because I have a boil on my bum.' No further questions were ever asked.

If only I had thought of this inventive pretext when I had been invited to the disastrous inauguration. Often, the ability to say no boils down to not just a carbuncle but also having a well-rehearsed, unverifiable excuse.

5

EK THA TIGER

It took a few years but eventually Mummy ji and I grew to appreciate and respect each other. I can say this with some certainty because she would often say, 'Hun you have become very good.'

Considering the word 'hun' in Punjabi means 'now', and she had been saying this for over ten years, I have never been sure at what point I went from Geeta to Seeta. Nor am I certain when her status changed from 'Aunty' to 'Mummy' in my head.

Mummy ji was an independent, outspoken woman. Not unlike me. This led to many situations where the man of the house once confessed, 'I feel sandwiched between you two.'

I comforted him by saying, 'Well, then you get to be the fancy avocado filling, while Mummy ji and I are just boring slices of bread.'

But Mummy ji, God bless her soul, despite living a seemingly monotonous life – home all day, gymkhana for her cards every evening – was as far from boring as Scotch is from urine. This is a fact exemplified by the day I am about to recount, when she turned perfectly mundane events into a memory that refuses to fade.

9 a.m.: I'm sitting on the floor of my workshop, arguing with the carpenter about the crow-shaped finials on a half-completed towering chair when my phone rings. It is Kanchan Masi, my mother-in-law's favourite cousin, who has just arrived from Chandigarh with her family and would like to come to my house for tea. I hastily tell her, 'Masi ji, I won't be home till 7 today. I would have

invited you over for lunch but my cook is on leave and you know how terrible I am in the kitchen!' And I hang up with a sigh of relief.

Ten minutes later, my phone rings again. It is Mummy ji. 'Kanchan told me you have invited them for lunch. How sweet! And don't worry, I am sending Ram Singh down to your kitchen, he will make all of Kanchan's favourite things. One more thing, Beta, if you have a little paunch, will you wear a ghagra choli or cover it up in a salwar kameez?'

I reply, 'I guess a salwar kameez,' wondering why Mummy ji has suddenly started asking me for fashion tips.

She says, 'Yes, that is exactly what I am saying. Why tell people you can't cook? Just like a big stomach, cover up your defects, Beta, no need to reveal all to everyone.'

12 p.m.: I walk into the kitchen to see Mummy ji's cook lording over my staff, especially Desi Jeeves. Recently, he had been unwell. Despite a barrage of blood tests, which did not give us any startling

insights aside from the fact that his haemoglobin levels are significantly higher than mine, Desi Jeeves decided that his health would improve only if he went back to his village for a few weeks. Now that he is back and claims to be 'first class, Didi', I ask him about his treatment. 'I went to Mangesh Baba. He hit me with a broom, and in five days, all sickness gone,' he tells me.

I make a mental note that the next time he is ill, we can save on doctor's bills as he can just request the watchman to clobber him with the vacuum cleaner so that he gets better even more swiftly.

1 p.m.: When my guests arrive, Kanchan ji's husband, who seems to strongly believe in vastu, tells me, 'The steps to your house are over a fishpond, a sunken area. See, that is the place from where Lakshmi Maa enters the home, and you have put an obstacle in her way.'

Disgruntled, because I really like my fishpond and now Mummy ji may just take up this 'demolition' as her next pet project, I mutter, 'It doesn't seem to stop people entering my house at the drop of a hat, so I am sure Lakshmi Maa will also manage to saunter in without falling into the fishpond.' A withering look from my mother-in-law and I quickly add, 'Some more palak paneer, Uncle ji?'

3.30 p.m.: I have a massive headache and am frothing and snarling at the prodigal son, when he peers at me and asks why I am behaving like the lead in *The Exorcist*.

I tell him, 'I don't know what is happening, but you may be right, I really feel like I am possessed by an evil spirit.'

He knows me a little too well and says that though there may be a slight chance that my salvation may lie with a crucifix-wielding priest, I should stop trying to diet today and try eating some carbs first. Sick of salads and craving spaghetti, I concede defeat and call my local baniya, 'Bhaisaab, please send two packets of Delverde organic spaghetti.'

He replies, 'Out of stock, Madam. Will you try noodles? Then, Maggi? If no, then try new Baba Ramdev's atta noodles, it's very good.'

So I ask him the most obvious question, 'Is this also a 2-minute noodle?'

And pat comes the reply, 'No madam, it is better. Three-minute noodle and bigger packet also.'

Now, though every woman will tell you that size does indeed matter and every extra minute counts, I decide to skip Baba Ramdev's offerings and eat leftover parathas.

6 p.m.: Mummy ji is playing cards with the prodigal son while I am oscillating between being an avid spectator and surreptitiously answering emails.

She stops dealing and, looking at her grandson fidgeting with his phone, says, 'Beta, are you also on that Snap talk thing?'

He replies, 'Snapchat, Granny, you want me to install it for you? You can send Snapchat stories to Pommi Bua in Delhi. See how much easier it is now that I have taught both of you to make WhatsApp video calls; this will be even more fun!'

I don't have the heart to tell the prodigal son that despite his detailed instructions, Pommi Bua still can't tell the difference between an audio and a video call. Last week, she swung open the bathroom door and passed the phone to her seventy-two-year-old husband while he was reaching for a towel, 'Mohan ji take this, Didi is calling from Bombay to wish you happy birthday!' At which point my mother-in-law promptly hung up as she had more than her fill of Mohan ji looking resplendent in his wrinkled but squeaky-clean birthday suit.

Probably recalling the same incident, Mummy ji shudders. 'Thank you, Beta, but I think we will just stick to normal phone calls.'

I bring up the topic of Desi Jeeves and his miraculous cure and Mummy ji nods enthusiastically, 'Yes, if you have devotion in your heart, you will find miracles everywhere. Once I remember Asha Bhen ji brought bottles of water from that full-of-sewage Mahim Creek, and started distributing it to everyone as prasad. She handed me a bottle and said, "Miracle water

Bhen ji, sea water has become sweet. Hundreds of people are drinking the water and jumping into the creek. Ganga Maa has come to us herself! But you don't have to go anywhere for this jal because I have got it for you".'

'Was it really sweet, Mummy ji?'

'I didn't try it, Beta! At the club I only like to take a little Thums Up. So I told her, "No thank you, Asha Bhen ji," and she made a face and said, "Mention not." Thank God, Beta, because I don't know what boon Asha Bhen ji got after drinking that water, but she did get acute dysentery.'

I reply, 'Mummy ji, we expend so much time, energy and, yes, money in trying to appease invisible entities with exacting rituals that we become credulous about anything and everything! At the end of the day it is all fear, isn't it? Fear of having nothing to rely on except ourselves. Fear is why we place all these godmen on towering pedestals.' I add with a laugh, 'In our country, it is difficult to walk on the roads without falling into a pothole or bumping into a holy baba, and honestly, the end result is pretty much the same.

Religion and superstition come in a "Buy 1 and get 2 free" policy but eventually pop up the existential question, are we limping because of the pain or because of the crutch?'

Mummy ji rolls the dice and says, 'Beta, some good advice, stop using so many big, big words or no one will come and sit next to you at parties. But you are right! No crutches and no limping for me!'

I sip my tea, grateful that I have a mother-in-law who is on the same page as me, and she adds, 'Because Beta, you see, after my knee replacement surgery, I toh am fully pain free!'

Mummy ji once told me that two tigers cannot live in the same field. By tigers, she was of course referring to the two of us. Fortunately, it turned out to be a false prophecy. We lived peacefully on the same premises for over twenty years till our dual stories turned into Salman Khan movie titles: 'Ek Tha Tiger' and 'Tiger Zinda Hai'.

Hun, the field, as she called it, is a lonely place.

6

THE JOYS OF MIDLIFE DOSTI

An old friend stayed with me last month. When it was time for her to leave, we hugged each other and I said, 'After five days, friends and fish both start to smell. You are leaving just in time.' My cousin, standing with us, took offence on her behalf. It was difficult to explain to him that this was a long-standing joke between us; old friends develop a language of their own, a Morse code of jests and jibes only they can decode. The joke started when we were in our thirties and, at that point in our rushed, harried lives, held an element of truth. Now, it seems to work as a defence mechanism against our sadness at having less time together.

As young women, our friendships are forged with lightning speed and held together with deep intensity. When I had just returned from boarding school, a tall eighteen-year-old with a laughter-filled nasal voice decided to make me her best friend. My loneliness evaporated in her steamy dining room; the table always laden with dishes left over from her mother's cooking classes. Our friendship had its bespoke fragrance – a mix of strawberry lip gloss, tandoori masala, spearmint chewing gum and, sometimes, sour hangovers. Boyfriends and breakups were minor creases quickly ironed out by the warmth of our friendship. We were leaving the family nest, ready for clumsy take-offs.

Relationships in our teens and twenties tend to be governed by identity formation. Like being in a room where mirrors are placed opposite each other, creating a series of endless reflections. Around another group of teenagers,

I felt awkward, always a step behind, but around my best friend, I was the best version of myself, the funny girl with a spirit that matched her large bottom. The greatest friendships fill all your hollow cavities like tides carrying seawater over sandy depressions.

In my thirties, friendships took on a different pattern. Earthshine is a lunar phenomenon, where the dark side of the moon is lit by a radiant crescent like a lopsided grin. I knew my friends existed, but most had been relegated to the background with just a sliver shining bright. During this phase, 'hold' seemed like a constantly used phrase: holding down jobs, holding together marriages and holding onto children. The days of bar crawling were replaced with couple dinners and Sunday brunches with the in-laws. Tasks and to-do lists were like termites burrowing into the yellowing fabric of our friendships, sometimes destroying them or, at best, turning them into safety nets that caught us as we fell. Friendships revolved around being the repository of each other's secrets with passcodes that could never be shared. Time was carved out for our close pals, but we were far from sitting in the sidecar and singing a duet about dosti like Jai and Veeru.

Then along came creaky middle age. Juggling work and home had become effortless after decades of practice, and some of us were also grappling with the empty nest syndrome. Our mothers had started playing rummy with their friends when they had reached middle age. Mine had a folding card table stacked in her garage, ready to be set up between her shoots and other engagements. Since playing rummy would further validate the frightening thought that we had truly turned into our mummy, my friends and I started playing board games, mahjong being the latest entrant on this list.

It's not that we suddenly have all the time in the world; it comes from knowing time is running out. It's not just the women; I also see my husband starting to schedule weekly volleyball matches with the same focus that he fixes his shoots. While I am guilty of merely moving meetings for our game get-togethers, the last time we played mahjong, one of my friends got off an eight-hour flight and headed straight to the table set up in my house. The dedication reserved for our children is now being used to service our needs for companionship.

A few weeks ago, we went bowling. Chomping on French fries and trying to knock down pins, it didn't feel very different from the days when we played pitthu and aimed at a pile of stones. The excitement at a strike, the groans when the ball went into the gutter and cheers for each other were reminiscent of our times on the playground. I lost the first game, and my friend suggested using a heavier ball. I protested, 'No, you know how weak my joints are; I don't have Popeye's biceps.' She insisted I give it a try. I did, and I won. From zero to hero. This was the same woman who, in my thirties, had pushed me to stop shying away from the limelight.

My identity is no longer shaped by my friends, yet in their gaze, I find traces of the best version of myself. These are old relationships based on trust. Ones that take time to blossom. Layers opening up in the Fibonacci spiral slowly over decades, like the strings of mogra I sometimes buy at traffic lights in the morning. Buds, white as a summer cloud, that will bloom by dusk.

Middle age has brought me back to the place my friends and I once inhabited on the threshold of adulthood. After years of being tied down with responsibilities, we are able to fly again. Swallows migrating together, wings spread out like origami fans, to the southern latitudes of our lives.

With time, you do get more comfortable in your skin, but that's because the poor thing is also not as tight as it used to be.

7

WHY THE VAMPIRE CHASED AMITABH, AND OTHER GHOSTLY (GHASTLY) JOKES

8.30 a.m.: We seem to celebrate every occasion with gusto. Come Diwali, there are diyas to be decorated and intricate rangolis on our porch. Every Christmas, the plastic tree is pulled out of storage and its droopy branches get Santa's version of Botox – good old tinsel stuffed into every crevice. And with Halloween around the corner, I am now getting ready for our annual dance with the devil. I'm sending e-invites to Miss Smarty Pants's friends when I am interrupted by the man of the house, 'Have you told the staff not to clean the hall?'

Mystified, I reply, 'Of course not, why would I?' Only to discover five minutes later that my Desi Jeeves has given everyone these instructions on my behalf.

Flashback: Two days ago, while sitting at my desk, I look up and see cobwebs. I call Desi Jeeves and point to the ceiling, 'There is a spider web in that corner!'

He looks up and says, 'Yes Didi! Should I remove it?'

Rolling my eyes, I say, 'Why bother? Let it grow bigger and bigger, and cover the whole ceiling so we save money on Halloween decorations.'

At which point, with a beaming smile, he walks away, not to get a stepladder as I had presumed, but to call a halt to all cleaning activities.

In the decade that he has been with me, Desi Jeeves has learnt some great things like driving a car, the art of downloading pirated movies onto his phone and some decidedly odd dance forms that he exhibits with great gusto during Ganesh Visarjan, while I have clearly still not learnt the greatest lesson – that sarcasm is wasted on him.

2 p.m.: Taking a break from work, I step out for a quick lunch with my cousin. Between morsels of palak paneer, I ask her if she has heard that a relative of ours has sprained his ankle by tripping over a pothole. She says, 'I did! And I told him that he should leave Mumbai and move to Madhya Pradesh. After all, their CM once claimed that the roads in MP are better than the ones in the US.'

I laugh. 'Some people cover their tracks while others I guess have to cover their potholes!'

'Covering tracks reminds me,' she says, 'do you remember when the government wanted to pass an ordinance that lets public servants hide their crimes and bribes?'

And then obviously realising that I am zoning out, she says, 'Acha, forget all this and listen to what I got as a forward this morning: "What advice did the ghost give his politician son? Beta, never become transparent like me.'"

4.30 p.m.: I can't find the pumpkin cutouts I had placed in the store room. I ask my helper, and she immediately blames Desi Jeeves, saying he misplaces everything. This is a change from when she had first joined us. I had noticed that Desi Jeeves had become rather friendly with her. I would spot her giggling at his remarks as they went around their daily chores. Then one afternoon, I came home unexpectedly and the kitchen door was locked. I huffed and I puffed and threatened to blow the door down, but it was a good five minutes before the door finally swung open. Desi Jeeves was standing by the fridge, and my young and married helper was leaning against the sink a few feet away. She instantly claimed that the door was jammed and that she was merely washing a glass.

Perhaps she was practising a unique method of water conservation because the sink was bone dry. Not one to spoil a happy romance, her marriage being her problem and none of my business, I made my cup of coffee and turned to leave when she blurted out, 'Don't mistake Didi, I have made him my brother!'

A month later, my heartbroken Man Friday, who had been her bhaiya in the living room and I assume saiyaan in the kitchen, had to part with both his paramour and two Dairy Milks while pretending to be thrilled at the prospect. Halloween is not the only celebration where you scare people. Sometimes Raksha Bandhan can be equally effective.

6 p.m.: In my eternal quest to lose weight, I have now stopped using the stationary bike parked on the first floor balcony as a clothes drying stand and have started using it for its real purpose. It's an allegory of life itself, as I frantically pedal, give it all my sweat, determination, hard work and still don't move forward an inch.

Desi Jeeves calls out to me from the garden below, 'Didi, there is a parcel for you. The man is saying you have to come and sign for it.'

I call out, 'You just sign for it please, who is it from?' and promptly he says, 'Amma Jaan!'

'Really?' I ask, as the name doesn't ring a bell. And he says, 'Haan Didi! It is written on the box!'

My brain going in circles faster than my legs, I mentally go through all my contacts, trying to find someone, anyone, who would fit the bill. Having once received a parcel filled with chopped-off hair as a declaration of deep love for the man of the house, I am cautious about accepting parcels from unknown people. I call out, 'Open it near the gate itself and tell me what's inside the box!'

A minute later he says, 'Didi, there is all jadu-tona things inside.'

Horrified, I get off my cycle and rush down to the gate. I gingerly peep inside the box and there I see it – a foam-filled skull decoration and not from any Amma Jaan but from Amazon. Good grief!

7.30 p.m.: Miss Smarty Pants is helping me hang up our decorations, little pumpkin lanterns on the trees and a string of felt bats over the main door. I try to get into the Halloween mood by regaling her with my very own ghostly or ghastly, whichever way you want to pronounce it, joke. 'Listen to this: Why did the vampire chase Amitabh Bachchan? Because he was allergic to all blood groups except AB. Why did the vampire not chase Abhishek Bachchan instead? Because our vampire is a connoisseur and AB, like fine wine, gets better with age. I think I really have a flair for this!'

My younger one, a rubber spider in her hand, protests, 'Mom, no, you don't. Bhaiya is right, your jokes are the worst.'

For most people, Count Dracula may only show up once a year on Halloween, but I am infinitely luckier as I have both my Desi Jeeves and Miss Smarty Pants sucking my blood all year round.

8

FIFTY SHADES OF BIGOTRY

Every summer I pack large suitcases for my small family, and we head off on a much-anticipated holiday. We usually end up on a beach somewhere, sand in our costumes, salt in our hair from the hazy blue sea, sunlight trapped in our skin. The grey monotone of city life is replaced by a palette of primary colours.

This year, I have the rare luxury of having the house all to myself as the family go on ahead to their holiday while I stay back to finish some writing. When it is time for me to join them, the man of the house informs me that certain things essential to his well-being have been left behind, and I must bring them along.

A day later, I find myself standing before a customs officer as he stares at the contents of my suitcase. 'Why do you have a thick wooden log in your bag?'

I hastily explain, 'It's not a log sir, it's a mudgal!'

'A what?' he asks.

'It's an ancient Indian way of weight training. You sort of hold it up in the air and whirl it around your head.' Though all I want to do at this point is knock the man of the house on the head with it. Why can't he, like most other movie stars, just go to the gym, take steroids and grunt over a chest-press machine instead of trying to recreate a Mahabharat-style akhara is beyond my comprehension.

But the angst is forgotten as I reach the sleepy and serene island. After months of being chained to my desk, physically present though mentally far away, I leave the world of words behind and re-enter the real one. I want to dance with my family, play board games and talk to them again.

Guilt is the interfering, strident Bua whispering inside every working mother's head, and now I am determined to make up for lost time. I end each night by reading to Miss Smarty Pants. I have never read her fairy tales, though. These are dangerous stories. There is always a beautiful and helpless princess waiting for a prince to rescue her. If that is not bad enough, there are characters like Cinderella who need MAC makeovers and shoes by Jimmy Choo to be perfectly happy. But my pet peeve is the mirror, mirror on the wall, who is the fairest of us all, Snow White. While I may refuse to hand this poisoned apple to my children, there are many other places where they will pick up on these subversive notions – in cartoons, from friends, and even from families who compare skin tones of siblings, or child and parent. This internalised bias based on colour has led to a lot of unhappiness, and an empire of skin-lightening products worth 450 million dollars in India.

The following afternoon, I realise that I managed to bring all of the man of the house's cumbersome items but have forgotten my shorts. So I head for a little store on the island to try on a few pairs. There is a long-legged woman around my age in the adjoining changing room and soon, we begin taking each other's opinions on the stuff we are trying on. When I change back into my own clothes, my fellow shopper with a strong British accent asks me where I got my dress. 'Cape Town,' I reply, and she smiles, 'Oh, I'm originally from Cape Town.' We start talking about our favourite restaurants and South African wines.

Then she comes close to my ear and whispers, 'Isn't it awful, what is happening there?'

'Yes,' I nod, 'the water crisis!'

She says, 'No, I mean the way the Blacks at the hospital are refusing to treat the poor White people. They should be grateful that they even have hospitals; after all, it's only because of us.'

I instantly realise two things. One, that despite our recent camaraderie, we have absolutely nothing in common, and two, she has only shared this with me because she thinks, like her and almost everyone on this island, I'm White. Us against them. Colour, a welcoming handshake at the entrance of bigotry.

On our last day on the island, cramped in the back of the car, I am rubbing sunblock on Miss Smarty Pants. She takes just a smidgen, and then pointing at her significantly paler brother who is now fifty shades of painful red, she claims, 'I don't need as much sunblock as him. My brown skin is stronger.'

I recall a time when she was younger and came to me saying she didn't want to take swimming lessons because she didn't like getting dark in the sun. 'I want to be the same colour as Bhaiya.' A chance remark by a foolish relative within her earshot, 'She is so cute but not as fair as her brother na!' had not gone unnoticed. And this led to many questions within our home about colour, with me telling her I want to be orange, the colour of her favourite carrots, and she laughing and wanting to be orange as well.

I asked her why brown is stronger and she replies rather proudly. 'White is a light colour so it gets dirty fast like my T-shirt. Brown is darker, so it doesn't,' is her simple explanation.

'Okay missy,' I say, 'I am giving you ten on ten for your analogy, but unfortunately you can't get out of using sunblock, you need it as much as him.'

I am far from the perfect mother. I cannot pick her up from school every day, and I spend too much time at my desk or, God knows, sometimes even on my nails, but somehow, I have managed, if not to keep all the balls in the air then to at least pick up dropped ones fast enough. In a world of fairness creams, racism, pale-skinned dolls and poison-filled fairy tales, my twelve-year-old is turning out to be a little girl who is perfectly comfortable in her own skin.

Witches were once princesses
who got tired of their
knights in shining armour
falling off their high horses
once too often, and finally
decided to take matters into
their own hands.

9

LEARNING TO LOVE DOGGY STYLE

We live in different tenses, my dog and I. Cleo bounds around in the only one she knows, the present, while I meander in the past as we circle endlessly around the garden. The Earth and her satellite treating a patch of grass as the centre of their solar system.

There are dogs who have been trained to do all sorts of tricks. Like the infamous Pidi who once took over Rahul Gandhi's X handle, declaring that he was the mastermind who tweeted for him. In the accompanying video, the super dog was seen doing namaste and balancing a biscuit on his nose. This was not a dog that ate the master's homework but instead did the homework for him.

Cleo doesn't believe in playing jester. To raise her paw for a delicate handshake is beneath her. Instead, she has trained me to play fetch. I throw a ball, she grabs it and then chews on it, waiting for me to walk over and pick it up.

A decade has passed in much the same way. Throwing balls, setting out bowls of food, occasionally dropping fleas into a kerosene-filled steel cup when she brings along blood-sucking playmates. Ticks may repel some people, but for me, they bring along a wave of nostalgia. My memories, leached of colour like the photographs I have left of that period, consist of sitting on a flight of stairs, my grandmother oiling my hair while my hands are busy picking out fleas from the furry creature lying by my feet.

Cleo's predecessor, Caesar, like his human counterpart, was a legend, albeit only in my household. On a stormy day, a cousin was lazing in a hammock. Caesar barked repeatedly and began grabbing the macrame knots with his teeth. Fed up, the little boy scurried off, moments before a coconut tree collapsed onto the hammock.

Regardless of whether Caesar could sense a threat or he just didn't like pesky kids, dogs in our household have been treated with reverence ever since. Cleo, in comparison, has not achieved any notable feats – aside from being named in a complaint for trying to bite a trespassing, nosy neighbour. At which point, I was almost tempted to file a counter case against the neighbour for violating my dog's olfactory space by regularly stinking of methi theplas.

Despite Cleo's lack of accomplishments, I feel a deep affection for her. A rare sense of contentment when I pat her on the head or brush her fur. This is not an unrequited emotion, according to scientists.

Researchers at Azabu University studied the role of oxytocin, the hormone responsible for bonding between humans, especially between mothers and babies. When asked to gaze into each other's eyes, dogs experienced a 130 per cent rise in oxytocin levels, and owners a 300 per cent increase.

We can still use objective reasoning over why our canine companions love us. Humans do provide food, shelter and protection, but it doesn't explain why we are so attached to our pets as well.

Perhaps it is as simple as what the fox tells the little prince in the eponymous book, 'I have no need of you. And you, on your part, have no need of me. To you I am nothing more than a fox like a hundred thousand other foxes. But if you tame me, then we shall need each other. To me, you will be unique in all the world. To you, I shall be unique in all the world.'

We take another round and I throw her a withered coconut. She chases it and, clamping it between her jaws, she lies down on the grass. While Cleo has clearly not learnt any tricks from me, I learn many just by watching her. Seeing her bound up to the people she loves, I am trying to let my guard down. There is an openness in our pets that we deny ourselves with our walls and defence mechanisms. A dog will see you and jump up and wag his tail, slobber all over your face. He doesn't stop to think, but does this person really like me? Will I be taken advantage of if I show him an abundance of affection?

When I spot her now flipping over onto her back, her belly facing the sky, living in the moment as prescribed by ancient religious tenets and new-age gurus, I want to emulate her. Use only my eyes, nose and ears while abandoning the reasoning brain. Lie flat on the grass without worrying about dirt, time and propriety, till buoyant bubbles of joy fill up all my crevices and cavities and burst in my chest.

I call out her name and she dashes towards me with a crow's carcass in her mouth instead of the coconut. I hold up her face, wanting to reprimand her, but as I look into her eyes, the colour of molasses and roasted cacao, I feel a sudden surge of emotion. It becomes clearer, the reason why we unzip secret compartments of our heart in order to carefully tuck these creatures inside.

It is the way our dogs look at us. It doesn't matter if we are adolescents or grandmothers, comely or plain, hilarious or terrible bores. Their gaze is a place without judgement. Dogs, with their paws, tails and snouts, remind us that we are never more human than when we, like them, love unconditionally.

I pat her on the head and we continue taking our circles. A pair of two-legged and four-legged creatures who have managed to tame each other.

Happiness is an accident,
not a pursuit. It only collides
against you when you are
looking the other way.

10

ADULT FRIENDSHIPS ARE SO HARD, YAAR. PINKY SWEAR!

Week 1: It's my second day at university, and I'm sitting alone at my desk, eating leftover orange peel. The astringent tang, with its stubborn strands of pith, feels like a perfect metaphor for my mental state after waiting in vain for one of my classmates – even the one with toothpaste all over his scarf – to suggest lunch during the break.

When I decided to return to university for my Master's in writing – a move that meant relocating to London, finding a school for my younger one and a home for all of us – I was prepared for logistical headaches. What no one warned me about was how hard it would be to make friends as an adult. Needing guidance, I call my mother from the empty classroom. 'Mom, did I make friends easily in school?' I ask.

She sighs. 'Well, you used to beat them into becoming friends with you. I remember you broke that boy's teeth – luckily they were milk teeth, so he didn't need fake ones. Remember Kabir? He was Farhan Akhtar's cousin. Then you beat Farhan too. And that time you went around threatening Amjad Khan's son until he became your friend. Then he used to get you a Thums Up 500 every day to share.'

At nearly fifty, I can't very well go around punching twenty-five-year-olds into friendship. Clearly, a new tactic is required, preferably one that doesn't involve dental work.

Week 2: Our dining table has been turned into a giant desk. The prodigal son, Miss Smarty Pants and I each have claimed a spot where we sit together and do our respective homework every evening.

While my older one has been in the UK for a few years now and has somehow acquired a large circle of friends who presumably have poor judgement, I am worried about my younger one. Uprooting her from Mumbai to London was not an easy decision. I know she has been homesick, missing her dog, her dad and the extended family, though not exactly in that order. I ask her about her new school, and with a wide grin she says, 'I spent all my breaks playing tag.' I am then informed that tag is a great game, especially when you have a gassy stomach, as you can run far and fart, and that she had received this information from one of her new friends.

When it comes to friendships, children seem to boisterously dive in and splash away, but we hold onto the pool ladder, submerging ourselves one step at a time while constantly checking the temperature.

Week 3: The professors have gone on strike because of budget cuts. I am secretly relieved as I dreaded having lunch alone in class once again. After making a head start on some of my course reading, which amounts to an average of two books a week, I decide that I might have to research some proven strategies if I wanted to be on the winning side of this friendship game. I soon come across a book on friendship by Marisa Franco, who suggests that people must actively pursue friends. While I had been staying away from making the first move because it made me feel like Betaal trying to clamber onto the backs of varied Vikrams, this information goads me into action.

That afternoon, I begin by chatting with my Irish neighbour while collecting our mail from the foyer table. Finn is an elderly man with hair sticking out of his head like a crow with mangy feathers and, like me, freshly unleashed upon London. 'Oh, you are from India!' he says. 'I have also recently moved from Dublin, and you know what – during this period, Boris Johnson got toppled, the Queen died, and now my old friends are asking what I will do to King Charles next.' Amused by his joke about the uneasiness between the British and the Irish, I suggested the adult, sedentary version of tag – coffee.

Week 5: The strike has been called off. Back in the classroom, I try to make eye contact and smile tentatively at my classmates, but aside from a bespectacled man next to me telling me I have a piece of spinach in my teeth, no one responds. Then the professor asks us to do a critical analysis and make a presentation on a few books. Graham Greene's *The End of the Affair* is on the list and I immediately put my hand up. Three other women have raised their hands as well. We are asked to form a group and do a joint presentation. That afternoon, one of the girls suggests that we spend our lunch break at a café opposite the campus and go over how we want to divide our project. Over bad dim sums and suspicious-looking prawn udon we first talk about our professors and then, our lives.

Week 6: Finn is over for another cup of coffee when our neighbour in the flat above makes a ruckus loud enough for us to peer out from our doorway. Finn asks me, 'Do you know who that is? He was engaged to a famous actress; she was in that *Princess Bride* movie. He pulled off a big scam and went to prison for a few years.'

'Finn, let's go meet him,' I say, 'Who knows, I could get an interview or even a great short story out of it!'

We devise methods of engineering an encounter with the former criminal till Finn confesses, 'This reminds me of when I helped a journalist with information about some Russians running a visa scam. He got a great story. They did cut off his little finger, but I suppose it was worth it.'

While my pinky is a rather useless appendage, I have become fond of it over the years, so I tell him I am having second thoughts about undertaking this particular mission.

That evening, I take the initiative and form a WhatsApp group with my three classmates. We try out names for our group and after shooting down a suggestion by the youngest member who appears to be smitten with our seventy-year-old, Dustin Hoffman-look-alike professor and insists on christening our group 'Blake's Bitches', we come up with the more sedate 'Scribes in the City'.

Week 7: We've left the key to our apartment inside. I am standing on the pavement, debating whether to call a locksmith, when the prodigal son suggests climbing in through the back window. Apparently, along with forgetting to bring the key, he'd also forgotten to lock the windows.

He hoists Miss Smarty Pants onto his shoulders, and she scrambles onto the window sill. I try to ignore the curious looks from passersby as she shoves the window up with all her might, slips inside, and immediately triggers a chorus of screeching alarms. In our enthusiasm for breaking into our own home, we'd neglected to disarm the system from our app.

Finn comes running out and is reassured that the only burglars on the block are already in conversation with him. Once Miss Smarty Pants graciously unlocks the door, I invite him in, and we drift into a discussion of his true obsession: the royal family.

He begins with an old tabloid relic: a curious bedtime conversation between Camilla Parker-Bowles and Prince Charles, during which His Royal Highness professed a desire to 'live inside her trousers' and be reborn as her tampon.

The prodigal son is lurking about. I tell him to finish his overdue assignment. He replies, 'You keep telling me to be ambitious and work hard, but look at Charles. His ambition was just to be a tampon, and now he's King.'

Finn, delighted by the prodigal son's joke, informs me that our nefarious upstairs neighbour is currently in and suggests we grab a bottle of wine to make our introductions. I decline, explaining I have guests coming over, though truthfully, I'd rather have a finger hanging off my palm than in every pie.

After Finn leaves, I start tidying for my afternoon tea with the Scribes in the City. We usually meet for lunch at uni, but sometimes defect to the pub or each other's homes.

At fifty, I can hardly believe I've got a college gang of like-minded women I can badger about citation rules while chewing cafeteria sandwiches.

Today the girls are in a raucous mood, swapping gossip between bites of scones. One story involves a classmate who lives on a houseboat and appears to be stoned in every seminar; another concerns a poet who is convinced she's Goldsmiths's Sylvia Plath – minus the talent, but with a tragic wardrobe.

That evening, as I clear up, I realise that by making the first move, I'm not riding on anyone's back, but I've rid myself of the weight on mine: the fear of rejection. In the past few weeks, I've befriended my younger one's school mums, chatted with neighbours, turned acquaintances into friends and built a small support system. It doesn't replace my family and friends back home, but it keeps me in good spirits.

I've also found that not taking rejection personally helps. As does planning a repetitive activity. Join a book club, or even a cult with weekly meetings, if you're partial to white bedsheets with eye holes, as long as it offers multiple chances for engagement. Having the same courses means I see my uni group regularly; with others, I fix weekly walks in the park or trips to new exhibitions.

After the first few months, I had to concede that making friends as an adult is similar to being asked to play Scrabble with only consonants. You have to make an effort till you get into the rhythm (which is a vowel-free word in case you do need to play this version).

After all, there is no point in having a stand-up act with the best lines in town if you have a row of empty seats facing you.

Evolution has programmed us to be afraid – of the dark, strangers, changes and even love. We open doors to our hearts because we are compelled. But not completely. We hold it ajar. Unable to step out. Hinges crusted with past scabs, the door needs a firm push. We wait. The sun sets without us revelling in its light. Push the door, ignore the screeching hinges, love with all your heart, love generously, fearlessly, in dollops and not dribs.

11

SATURDAY NIGHT FEVER AND THE GAME OF STAYIN' ALIVE

9.30 a.m.: I want to sit by the window with my coffee and continue staring at a boat cutting across the still ocean with a plume of shimmering ripples and scavenging birds, but I have an urgent to-do list. It starts with managing my portfolio, which, thanks to Trump's tariffs, is making me see red, figuratively and on the trading app. I message my accountant, and while waiting for her to reply, I start jotting down a weekly menu for the family.

I can't cook, nor do I have an avid interest in food besides soya chaklis. Yet, this menu planning is by default my department until I die or, if I am lucky, get dementia and can't recall anyone's favourite dishes. My phone pings – it's not my accountant but the kind folks at Myntra informing me that I can avail of their 46 per cent Happy Women's Day discount on a black seamless tummy and thigh shaper.

While there is merit in acknowledging the progress women have made by having a dedicated day to celebrate our wins, sometimes it does feel like a relay race. Every generation passes the baton forward, only to find the next leg of the race is also uphill; we are dressed in shaping underwear and stilettos and are still underpaid.

1 p.m.: At lunch with my sister, I decline dessert. 'I don't want Saturday night me short-changing the Sunday morning me,' I tell her.

She frowns. 'Are you stoned? What the hell does that even mean?'

'We indulge our Saturday night versions, by

which I mean our present selves, and leave our future or Sunday morning versions to clean up the mess,' I reply. 'One drinks, the other suffers. One binges, the other repents.'

When she looks puzzled, I tell her about *The Substance*, the Demi Moore horror movie that changed my perspective. A washed-up ageing actress injects herself with a green serum that spawns a younger, better version of herself. They are supposed to time-share their existence, seven days in each body. 'Remember you are one,' the serum dealer warns them. But the younger one keeps overstaying, partying and draining the other older body, which rapidly decays.

The film is about ageing and the societal pressure on women's bodies and self-worth. The absolute horror for me was seeing the two bodies side by side and the immediate effects of what we do to our future selves daily: the extra drink, the midnight cake, the 'just one more episode' binge.

'Whenever temptation strikes, I tell myself that the Saturday night me and Sunday morning me are one. It stops me in my tracks.'

'Can I tell you the truth?' my sister says. 'Every version of you, including this Friday afternoon one, is a big bore.'

3 p.m.: On the way back to the office, Instagram pops up an old video of the Trump and Zelensky showdown. The Ukrainian president had found himself in an uncomfortable situation at the White House where he was grilled on his lack of a suit, talked down to like a preschooler, and expected to show the same level of gratitude that Trump saves for his beloved hairspray that, fittingly, is called CHI Helmet Hair. As women, we are often in rooms with uneven power dynamics. If Zelensky had asked for advice, I would have told him the first rule of survival in a lopsided negotiation: Always state your case like you're threading a needle – steady and careful, trying not to prick your finger in the process.

6 p.m.: I coax Miss Smarty Pants into playing football at a neighbouring compound. She returns earlier than expected, saying that the older kids

were cheating. I try explaining that sometimes things may not be to our liking, but the game goes on and so do we. When she continues whining, I threaten to ground her.

'I will ground you instead,' she says and orders me to go and stand on our garden stoop. Trying to lighten the mood, I climb up and say, 'It's cool because I am used to being on a pedestal.'

She replies, 'If you want to be on a higher pedestal, then just climb up your ego.'

Her sarcastic retort both dismays and amazes me. Unlike in the movies, I suppose you don't need to inject a green serum into your veins to spawn a younger, better version of yourself.

9 p.m.: I scroll through the photo library on my phone and see pictures from my recent trip to Kolkata. Some are taken at Kumartuli, where artisans craft stunning idols for Durga Puja. It's a fascinating process that starts with a wood-and-straw skeleton before adding layers of clay. The guide who took me to see the artisans at work said that traditionally, women were restricted from

practising this craft. An irony that women, despite being the embodiment of Goddess Durga, are now fighting for their place in crafting her image.

I suppose life's scales have always been rigged. A fortunate few get to choose how to live; others have to choose what they can live with.

Whether you are a president fighting for your country's survival, a kid on a playground or a woman looking at equality that lasts beyond a perfunctory celebration, this holds true. We don't have control over the outcome of any of these games besides the one we play with ourselves daily. The tug of war between our present and future selves – between impulse and restraint, indulgence and wisdom. Well, unless you are an anomaly like Donald Trump, whose Saturday night avatar revels in junk food, lawsuits, temper tantrums, and yet his Sunday morning version – defying Newton's third law of motion that for every action there is an opposite and equal reaction – pats him on his head and even fixes his hair in place as he keeps stomping on.

Heels are empowering only if you mistake altitude for attitude. If heels were truly powerful, then wouldn't men be wearing them as well? Jeff Bezos on the cover of *Time* magazine in Jimmy Choo peep toes. Elon Musk driving his Tesla in Versace stilettos. Putin posing bare-chested with a hunting gun and Manolo spike heels.

12

CHIPPED TEACUP

My friends lost their son. When I heard about it, I felt like I had caught my hand in a door. An unexpected wrenching pain that dulled after a while but left me aching and bruised.

A teenager. With his father's smile, one that didn't curve at the ends but lit up his face in a broad horizontal line. An incipient moustache watched over that distinctive grin, an indicator of a boy about to turn into a man.

Death sometimes knocks at the door till it is opened, and at other times, it slips in unannounced. When my grandmother, who had a large hand in raising me, passed away, sorrow felt like the needle of a sewing machine. Piercing through and lifting rhythmically. Forgotten for a few moments, it would slam down again. The salty Mumbai air suddenly heavy in my lungs, as if it were liquid going down the wrong pipe. Yet, there was a comfort in knowing she had lived a full life.

But even that meagre solace is absent when it's the demise of a child. It is the materialisation of every mother's greatest fear, one that we live with from the time we are aware of another heart beating inside us.

I recall an Emily Dickinson poem that has stayed with me over the years.

I measure every Grief I meet
With narrow, probing, eyes —
I wonder if it weighs like Mine —
Or has an Easier size.

Is there a more difficult version of grief to

carry than the death of a child? That unfulfilled promise and a lifetime of memories that should have been his right?

But loss does not bend to our will. Like the love that precedes it, it arrives unannounced. To love itself is to accept the inevitability of separation. One way or another. And yet we are always unprepared.

After I speak to the parents, I make a cup of tea, a familiar ritual of comfort. The ceramic cup clinking against another as it is pulled out. The kettle pretending to be a tone-deaf man whistling an unfamiliar tune. The trickle of water into the cup. A chip, the size of a molar. One I had not noticed before. The teabag gliding in. For a moment, it floats. Then drowns. Sinking to the bottom.

Submerged. It waits. I wait. At first it is imperceptible. The leaking of colour. Strongest at the centre. The smell, herbaceous, mint and molasses, riding on the rising steam. The teabag loses form and function. A paper husk fished out, discarded. I wonder if the tea bag, stacked with others, looked at this cardboard box with Twining's Tea emblazoned in capital words, as its world or a waiting room. When it slid into the cup, was it afraid of letting its essence disappear? Or did it know that it was not dissipating, only changing form, from a tea bag to a cup of tea?

It is the fourth day. A time when heartbroken families offer prayers. I watch a slideshow of pictures of the young boy. With his brothers, laughing with his friends, sitting on his mother's lap. I write to her. But what comfort can you give someone who must forget her dreams, erase the line of stars she had once seen strung up through her little one's eyes?

I make another cup of tea and I sit by the window. Grieving. For the beautiful boy with his father's smile. And for a loss that could just as easily have been mine.

Age is a mathematical problem. It is not a division sum though, where we are reduced to a fraction of what we once were. It is one of multiplication.

At forty, you are still the pigtailed girl who once climbed trees and beat up all the boys. The young woman with a disdain for convention. The new mother with leaky breasts and fierce ambition. You don't have one heartbreak, one breakdown, one true love, one success; you have a mountain of them.

Yet we look at our crinkled eyes, creaking knees, the loosening of skin as it detaches from muscles with despair. Instead, we should perhaps learn to honour our lines and folds, our aches and pains. The equivalent of a general's medals, pinned to our skin, a reminder of all the battles we have survived, and the ones we have won.

13

FROM FOIE GRAS TO BHEJA FRY

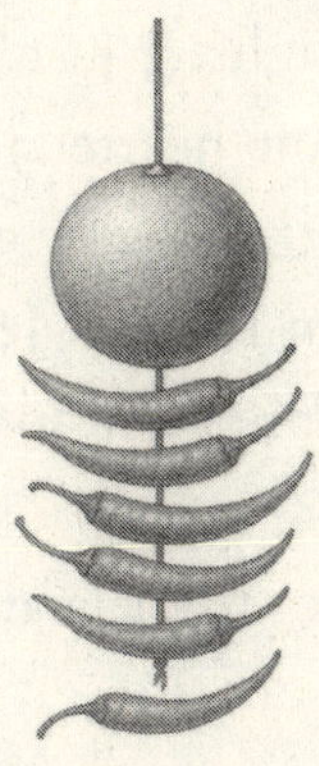

9 a.m.: Back from a holiday, my mind is refreshed and my stomach is stuffed with foie gras and French fries, but what I really craved for while in France was a masala dosa. Hoping to score one, I go into the kitchen, where I see Desi Jeeves hunched up near the refrigerator and ask him, 'You went to the doctor yesterday na? What did he say?'

He answers, 'Doctor said main halke dilwala hoon na.'

I call the doctor in bewilderment, 'Doctor, is this "halke dilwala" a medical diagnosis or are you just blurting out the title of Karan Johar's next blockbuster?'

Doctor Saab sighs. 'I just tried to explain to him that he is a faint-hearted fellow. Very anxious chap; has been getting panic attacks.'

I hang up, turn to Desi Jeeves and ask him, 'You were fine before I left, so what's with all this panic attack stuff?'

'No Didi, I went to mela and after that I have become like this.'

Can this be an underhand dig at me for my diabolically disastrous movie *Mela* or did he really go to some fair and get spooked? On further questioning, I get my answer. Apparently last month on his annual holiday, he sat on a giant wheel and somewhere between the sixth and the seventh round, he changed from a happy-go-lucky individual to this timorous wreck.

He continues his story by saying, 'Didi, jealous people are doing black magic on me. Can I go back to village this week? There is a good baba, you remember once he cured me before, only he can cure me again.'

I can fight against many things, but in front of superstition, I promptly accept defeat, so I hastily get him onto the next outbound train.

11.15 a.m.: I get a call from my factory supervisor, 'Madam, I can't come to office, my wife has lost her finger.'

Puzzled, I ask, 'Lost? As in, she kept it somewhere and can't find it? Or lost, as in, it fell off in her sleep?'

'No Madam, last night she wanted to put one more load in the washing machine as it is inauspicious to wash clothes on Thursday, so she had to finish it that night itself. She got up in the middle of the night to take the clothes out and put them to dry; and half asleep, she forgot to turn the machine off before putting her hand inside. The machine cut her finger off.

'Yes of course, take the day off,' I reply.

6.30 p.m.: I am at an old friend's house when her granny drops in for a visit. The old lady unrolls a piece of paper, points at it with her withered finger and tells my friend, 'Payal Beta, your horoscope says that you have been having bad luck for the last six months, and it will continue for the next year. You see, Saturn has entered your eighth house.

I try refuting this with simple logic. 'Aunty ji, Payal doesn't have eight houses, just this one in Juhu, so if Saturn is entering the eighth house it is definitely not hers.'

Granny glares at me and continues, 'I have a solution. I have asked Kaveri Amma in Chennai and she said that every Saturday for a month, Payal must feed a cow some grass. Then all the problems will be solved, Beta.'

My friend's reply – that she really doesn't have any problems – literally falls on deaf ears because Granny suddenly yelps, 'Arre, this hearing aid has started making beeping sounds. I can't hear anything! Change the battery for me, Payal!'

Battery all changed and Granny says, 'How many years do I have left to live? Can't you just listen to your dadi and make me happy before I die?'

After Granny leaves the room, Payal turns to me, saying, 'How can I say no to her now! Maybe she is right also. So for the next few Saturdays, you will see me near Mukteshwar Temple, running behind a cow with straw.'

I snort. 'Listen, why don't we update all these rituals and instead of feeding the cow, you start an initiative called #selfiewithcow and post a bunch of pictures – the new age way to thwart bad karma!'

'Stop talking crap!' she says.

I retort, 'Well, if your granny's prophecy of bad luck has to come true then it will only be because you are doing all these crazy things. You just may get arrested as a suspected beef addict, desperately trying to get her fix by luring the poor cow!'

France and Belgium may fight over the origin of the French fry but only we Indians have invented a delicacy called bheja fry. And at the rate that mine has been fried by mumbo-jumbo today, I may as well drive to Mohammad Ali Road and sell it with some pav.

But first, I must call up the man of the house and immediately register this movie title before one of the Khans usurps it and I see it plastered on hoardings all over. No, not 'Bheja Fry' – that has already been used as a movie title – but my newfound idiom, 'Main Halke Dilwala Hoon Na'.

Kindly refrain from judging me on the quality of the following words, this is a verbatim account of what a friend narrated during my informal survey.

Sharing a bowl of poha for breakfast, she was asked, 'Should I do potty before we eat this or after?'

Unfortunately, the question was not raised by her toddler, but by her thirty-eight-year-old husband. Braver than I am, she immediately called her mother-in-law, handed him the phone and said, 'Ask Mummy!'

14

HOW TO SURVIVE MARRIAGE WITHOUT GOING TO JAIL

Each Valentine's Day, an avalanche of vile, heart-shaped candy gets passed around, though what the women who have been imprisoned long enough within the gilded cages of matrimony really yearn for is a heavy-duty replacement. Husbands for some odd reason, after a year or so, just stop functioning efficiently. Unlike a refrigerator, they don't even come with any sort of extended warranty, so you are stuck with this creature who, from sweeping you off your feet, now grumbles when he has to lift his feet off the coffee table.

This notion hit me even harder when the man of the house was sprawled on the sofa, as we coached our daughter for her karate exam. My count of ichi, ni, san was interrupted with 'Wah! A chauka!' I first thought my black belt–wielding partner had forgotten the basics, 'San is three in Japanese and not four!' But I discovered that he was surreptitiously watching cricket on his iPad instead. It was then, ladies, that I wanted to punch him on the head, not hard enough to knock him unconscious – in the hope that like most electronics, a quick switch off and on would restore optimum functionality – but just to give him a headache in return for the one he frequently gave me.

I stopped mid-air when I recalled Lana Clayton's case. Clayton was sentenced to twenty-five years for murdering her husband with drinks laced with eyedrops. Her defence was that she didn't mean to kill him but wanted to merely make him uncomfortable.

I had my next eureka moment when I spoke to a friend that evening. She had had to watch her husband spend two hours playing games on his phone, and was thrilled when his phone crashed. Cackling away, she said, 'The phone has gone for repairs! God heard my prayers.'

Wondering why I needed to rely on God when I could try a DIY method, I got home and secretly changed the man of the house's iPad password. It is difficult to quantify the joy I felt that night, watching him enter his password repeatedly, till his device was disabled.

I then realised that it was possible to devise methods where we could fight back without fighting at all. Honestly, when you have kids, jobs, in-laws and pets, who has the time to indulge in bickering, sulking and then all the heart-to-heart discussions?

1. The haunted house method

His wallet mysteriously moves from his bedside to the bathroom, the car keys go into a drawer in the kitchen, his glasses are under the sofa. To make it even more perfect, the wife coos, 'Baby, either we have a poltergeist or you have become forgetful! Should we go to the doctor? Your bua also suffered from early Alzheimer's; it could be a genetic thing na?'

2. The use-it-or-lose-it tactical manoeuvre

Use his things liberally when he is not around. His shampoo, which is not good enough for your fabulous mane, can be used on your dog. Knot and wear his shirts and t-shirts to the gym or even gardening. His razor? Why have a Brazilian wax when you can leave wiry strands in his razor? Revenge is best served cold, and this one ensures that it is served at a hair-razing temperature.

3. Divert and deflect

When your partner is annoying you by talking about inane things or repeating the same story

3,000 times, refrain from throttling him. No judge will accept, 'Milord, I just wanted to choke him till he stopped talking, not till he ceased breathing!' Instead, ask him random questions so it breaks the loop in his head. Even something as stupid as, 'Is today an odd day or an even one?' Men have the attention span of goldfish; after trying to answer, he would have completely forgotten what he was talking about in the first place.

4. Whips, collars and commands

Though marriage does seem to involve a fair bit of domination and submission, it is usually accompanied by vanilla sex, so this isn't a call for some BDSM action. Watching our dog Freddie's trainer working with him, I noticed that he uses a simple method. He ignores Freddie's tantrums and gives him a treat when he displays appropriate behaviour. If you are highly motivated, this is a nifty method. Ignore him when he asks you to find his socks. Offer kisses and onion pakoras, in that order, as a reward for good behaviour. At the very least, it's more entertaining than watching him watch yet another cricket match.

5. Emulate Mummy ji

When the man of the house felt ill, off he would go to Mummy ji's house, claiming that her haldi doodh was a miracle cure. When I made the same in my kitchen, he dismissed it as ineffective. Swallowing my pride along with all the vile concoctions I had tried, I approached Mummy ji. She smiled, 'Beta, I drop two Crocins in his milk, bas, and he becomes fit and fine.'

This method can be handy even in sticky situations like a boys' night out. Instead of nagging him about not going, try saying, 'You work so hard and deserve to have some fun. Let's have a drink together before you head out, shall I get you a rum and Coke, darling?'

Out of sheer relief at escaping a battle of wills, he will agree. This is your chance to douse his drink, not with eyedrops, but with a big dose of a cough syrup like Benadryl that also causes drowsiness. Passing out was his plan anyway, you have just ensured that instead of the long route with multiple drinks and a late night, he takes a shortcut and passes out nice and early.

You may wonder, if your partner is so annoying, then isn't it better to just find another suitable mate? According to relationship coaches, being frequently irritated with your partner is normal. We just don't expect it to be part of an ideal relationship, as we have grown up on tales of happily ever after. All these stories, though, either stop at the grand wedding or, like Romeo and Juliet, have the protagonists die before they start bickering about smelly bathrooms.

The truth is that even if you could replace this pesky partner for another (this, of course, excludes violence and other deeply toxic behaviours, in which case, run as fast as you can), then it would only be exchanging one set of problems for another, as human beings are inherently flawed creatures.

The only way to survive a long-term relationship is to be pragmatic, accept differences and follow what Gibran advocated, 'Let there be spaces in your togetherness.' Since matrimony is also meant to be about sharing joy and sorrow, there is no real harm done in using the subversive tactics above, to give you some joy while causing him sorrow.

15

EXAM WARRIORS

While the prodigal son is now in university, getting him there was no small task. Like most mothers, I carried the weight of it alone. Eventually, I admitted I might need help. A friend kindly gave me Modi ji's book, *Exam Warriors*. I read it late one night, then tried to follow it the next morning. The day did not go quite as planned.

6.30 a.m.: Cleo is barking in the balcony and I jump out of bed and hurtle at P.T. Usha speed to muzzle my dog so she doesn't disturb the prodigal son. He is preparing for his IGCSE mock exams and, according to Modi ji's book, it is very important to be well-rested before tests. In fact, there is an entire chapter called 'Sleep is your greatest weapon, embrace it'.

7 a.m.: Black coffee, both literally and the Ella Fitzgerald musical version, is running through my system because sleep, the greatest weapon, self-destructed three-and-a-half hours ago. I am then informed, 'Driver has not come, Didi!' Spotting the man of the house exercising in the garden, I holler, 'Need to drop off the kids so come inside right now!' Pretending to be deaf, he immediately begins doing cartwheels in the opposite direction, so five minutes later, I find myself performing my own acrobatics behind the steering wheel.

7.25 a.m.: My eyelids feel like the rusty shutters of a godown, and I have to push with all my might to keep them open. Article 3 of the

Geneva Convention states that all prisoners must be treated humanely, and not tortured with techniques like induced psychosis and sleep deprivation. But motherhood is a biologically induced psychosis where detainees volunteer to get tortured for nine months while a parasitic organism, akin to a tapeworm, grows inside their body. And then feeling such extreme pain that it would be slightly easier to lie down in the middle of a highway and have a truck run over us, we expel a creature who often looks uncannily like our mother-in-law! Add a few years of extreme sleep deprivation and you have bone-tired women, convincing themselves in the same manner as victims of the Stockholm syndrome, that they have deep feelings of affection towards their two-foot-tall captors.

The prodigal son snorts, 'Mom! What are you babbling about?'

'Crap! Did I just say all that aloud?' I groan.

'Mama called you a tapeworm!' Miss Smarty Pants declares, and her brother retorts, 'You are two feet tall, so she is talking about you!'

Just as they get ready to scratch each other's eyes out, we luckily reach the school gates.

1 p.m.: At the store and about to grab lunch, I check my phone and discover the school moms' WhatsApp group is filled with frenzied messages. 'You need to get a tuition teacher who will check that they are properly revising all the subjects they don't have a tuition teacher for!'

And then, 'Must solve all the past IGCSE papers from 2002 onwards as revision!'

Another mom says, 'The only place they have a few sets of the papers left is Jatin Book Centre in Jogeshwari!'

And the chat goes completely silent. All the mothers are probably making a beeline for Jatin Bhai. I remember that *Exam Warriors* also states, 'Revise and become wise!' So I reluctantly push my lunch away and jump into the car. After an hour and a half, I triumphantly return with the towering sets, see fourteen missed calls and realise that in all my frenzy of fetching the papers from Jogeshwari, I have forgotten to fetch my daughter from school!

4.30 p.m.: My mother has agreed to take Miss Smarty Pants to her tennis class. I nervously ring her door bell, 'Thanks for this, Mom. One small thing, I scraped against your car, it was an accident!'

Mother sighs, 'So were you, Beta, and more than forty years later, I still seem to be paying for all the damages!'

Before she can berate me further, I hastily deposit my younger one in her arms and run down the stairs.

6 p.m.: I sleepwalk through two meetings when my assistant reminds me that she is taking a week off to help her daughter with her board exams. There is no point asking why her husband can't take some leaves and help their child instead. Raising children, keeping them clean and fed, doing school rounds and spending a minimum of ten years of our lives dressing the kids as Harry Potter, Mahatma Gandhi, Dracula, Peppa Pig and Chhota Bheem, all seem to be a woman's job, regardless of whether she is a stay-at-home

or a working mother. And if cinema is a reflection of culture, then do note that we made the iconic *Mother India* in 1957, and almost seventy years later, 'Father India' has not even been conceived, let alone unleashed on the silver screen!

7.30 p.m.: I get home and poke my head into the prodigal son's room, 'How are the revisions going? Have you solved the papers? I had to push some rather aggressive women out of the way to get them for you.'

He rolls his eyes, 'For God's sake, Mom, we have been solving them since August last year and I don't need any hard copies! It's available online at papacambridge.com.'

I am suddenly very offended, not because I missed my lunch, missed picking up my daughter from school and did not manage to miss the left bumper of my mother's car, but because the website for exam papers is called PAPA Cambridge.

How dare they! What do fathers have to do with education! Check any school WhatsApp group and you will hardly see any bearers of the precious XY chromosome.

The education game is the only place where we women are allowed (or rather, compelled since there are no other takers) to have a voice, in a world that largely wants us silent.

I roar, 'That's unfair, they should change the bloody name to Mama Cambridge! I am going to start a Change.org petition right now!'

'Err ... Mom, but could you now drop me to maths tuitions first?'

I wonder if these sort of expeditions were what Modi ji was referring to in Chapter 22 when he said, 'As one journey ends, another begins!'

I wearily follow the prodigal son down the stairs, saying, 'The real exam warriors are not students but their valiant mothers. I wish someone would write a book for us instead.'

Ignoring my rumbling stomach, I get into the driver's seat again.

16

HONEY, WE'VE SHRUNK THE KIDS BUT OUR STATUES ARE TALLER

11.45 a.m.: I am making insecticide by mixing sugar powder with boric acid when my mom calls, 'Biren Bhai is arriving from Surat today. Send the driver to fetch your uncle from the station.'

'My driver is on leave today and I can't go either! There is a nasty ant infestation at home that I am trying to get rid of.'

She replies, 'You should not kill ants, they are very lucky.'

'Yes, Mom,' I mutter, 'Ants are lucky, it's just people like me covered in bites who are unlucky.'

My protests are pushed aside and as usual, Mom manages to get me to do her bidding.

3 p.m.: Once Biren Bhai and his dabba of precious fafdas are safely ensconced in the car, he begins rattling away in great excitement. 'When are you coming to Gujarat? You have to come to see the Statue of Unity, not very expensive, only 350 rupees.'

I reply, 'I thought it cost 3,000 crore, no?'

'Dikri, that is for the full and final statue, this I am telling you is for the ticket for observation deck view.'

I reply, 'Biren Bhai, there was an article once in the *Daily Mail* filled with British outrage about the UK giving 1.17 billion pounds as aid to India and us spending around a third of that on erecting statues.'

My uncle gets annoyed, 'Amtha, amtha sawal nai puch. British people are all salo chors! They took billions from us and tucked it nicely in their khisu, now what they are giving is interest on our capital only.'

Finally, though, the four-and-a-half hours on Paschim Express take their toll and he nods off.

5 p.m.: Pulling out weeds in my garden, I look out at the tranquil Arabian Sea. If things go according to plan, soon enough I will be able to spot a 212 metre Shivaji statue rising from the waves.

I recall reading a story about a philosophy professor who filled an empty jar with rocks, and then asked his students if the jar was full. When the students nodded, he dropped pebbles inside which rolled in between the rocks. Then he poured sand and filled up the remaining areas of the jar. Using it as an analogy for well-being, he said, 'This jar represents your life. The rocks are the important things – your family and your health. The pebbles are other things that matter, like your job, your house. The sand is everything else, all the small stuff. If you put the sand into the jar first, then there is no room for the pebbles or the rocks.'

I wonder if we as a nation are focusing more on building sand castles in our jars, bypassing our pressing issues of poverty and pollution and putting resources into playing Statue Statue instead. But I suppose if that is the name of the game, then we may as well spend another few hundred crore to ensure that the world's tallest statues are made a tad more relevant by having the world's biggest anti-pollution masks sitting jauntily on their noses.

8 p.m.: Not only do I have ants running around my house looking for edible items but I also have relatives who are doing the same. My mother arrives with Biren Bhai, while the man of the house had invited all his five uncles. While Mother starts nagging me about how the hot snacks are apparently not hot enough, Biren Bhai has been discussing his new business venture with the mamas. On hearing snatches of their conversation, I am almost tempted to ask my uncle if the tallest statue in the world has inspired him to invest in this product he is now peddling called Dr Ayurveda Height Increaser. Vinay Mama reels off product details from Biren Bhai's phone: 'This

product increases height in humans. It has no side-effects and is approved by Medical Council of India.' He then adds with a laugh, 'Arre Biren Bhai, this is a foolish business idea! How can this work on adults? At our age the only direction we can grow in is sideways.'

Over the years, I have noticed that politics has affected our family on a deeply personal level. When Manmohan Singh was the prime minister, my in-laws, dancing to the tune of *Singh Is King*, would bully my meeker Gujarati relatives, but after Modi ji has taken over, the Gujjus are ready with snappy comebacks.

A belligerent Biren Bhai retorts, 'What do you know about business? Let me tell you all great businessmen in India – Ambani, Adani, Kotak – are all Gujarati! You people may have muscle power but we have brain power. My bapu ji always used to say, "In business, Sindhis sell and Punjabis buy, but the middle person who makes a profit is none other than a Gujarati."'

Unfortunately, since Biren Bhai has not begun consuming the Height Increaser pills, he is still considerably tinier than Vinay Mama. And before Mama ji turns him from a spongy khaman into a deflated thepla, the man of the house quickly leads him away.

I look at my mother and sigh, 'Don't feel bad, Mom, but really, Biren Bhai is the reason why I think ants are better than uncles.'

My poor pun doesn't land, so off I go to grab, if not the tallest, the largest drink I can get. Sometimes you do need to pour some Scotch on the rocks to fill your jar of well-being right up to the brim.

Online troll: 'You third-class person. You make jokes about God.'

Me: 'God clearly likes a good joke, otherwise She would not have made you.'

17

TEN NEW COMMANDMENTS, WITH THE AID OF ONE VIRGIN MARY AND TWO BLOODY ONES

New Year resolutions and mobile phones have one thing in common, they both run out of battery very rapidly, but more than half the population is still convinced they can change their lives from the first of January. This, in fact, is an unlucky date to begin anything. If you don't believe me, ask Pope Francis's ghost. Despite not drinking himself into oblivion on New Year's Eve, the late Pope Francis once had to start the year with an apology to the world for slapping away the hands of a woman who had grabbed his arm. Lesser mortals stuck to the resolutions they made – and broke – every year such as losing weight, exercising more, quitting smoking and spending more time with family.

Realising the urgent need for alternative resolutions, I first tried reaching out to the Dalai Lama for advice. After calling Dharamshala and being put on hold for so long that I wondered if they were waiting for His Holiness to be reincarnated before transferring the line, I decided to give it a go myself. With the aid of one Virgin Mary that soon led to two bloody ones, here is a list of some much-needed and fairly achievable resolutions.

1. Set the bar low

Setting the bar as low as possible also makes it easy to reach for a drink when you need it next. Begin by first accepting that you aren't going to lose twenty pounds this year just the way you didn't the year before that. So, plan to make small changes, like losing the four pounds you gained during Christmas, when taking it a step further from Jesus who turned water into wine, you did your own transmogrification by turning wine into cellulite.

2. Emulate Baba Twinkdev

One way of impressing people is to simply flourish impressive credentials, like adding a 'Dr' before your name. This is not as difficult as it seems. Instead of putting in arduous hours obtaining a PhD, you could apply to self-styled institutions like the Trinity College based in Spain, and with a cheque for 295 pounds, get a doctorate in twenty-eight days. If even that is too much effort, then do it the Indian way. Simply tag on an honorific like Yogi, Maa, Swami, Baba or Guru, and without having to display any real abilities, people will look at you with reverence.

3. Turn into a bad parent

This may horrify school moms across the country but the best parent is a bad one. In order to get ready for the real world, all children need a few hard knocks. Now for some, life does this automatically, but for the ones who are bubble-wrapped in privilege, it is up to the parent to provide the required kicks on a regular basis. And yes, fellow moms, it is bad enough that along with office work, we are also saddled with almost all the house work – let's not add sixth grade homework to that list.

4. Admit you are stupid

Contemplation of your own stupidity may be the most intelligent thing you can do. It is only the truly dumb who are convinced of their smartness. The ones who agonise over the fact that they are perhaps secretly idiots, are the ones who know that there is so much to know that they clearly don't know enough. Also, if you can understand that sentence, then you are clearly a moron like me, which in this case is also a prime example of an oxymoron.

5. Stick out like a sore thumb

Don't try to blend in. As someone who obviously played a lot of Tetris once said, 'If you fit in, you disappear.'

6. Resurrections are granted to the stubborn

My old friend Bobby Deol, who was once written off, is now referred to as Lord Bobby and has a massive fan base called 'Boobians'. Do you remember that famous line about God's house where there is der but not andher? At some point, we do reap the rewards of sticking it out. Well, unless it's the losing twenty kilo resolution because God clearly has better things to do than getting you into a size ten dress.

7. An asana a day

Hindu, Muslim, Sikh, Isai, we all need to do some yoga, bhai. Also resolve to abstain from such terrible rhymes.

8. Use the right weapon at the right time

You need to use a bullet against a tiger that is charging at you, not against a bee because you don't like its buzzing.

9. Cultivate a bad habit

You are a lot more likely to succeed if you replace one bad habit with another bad one. For example, what if you replaced cigarettes with the healthier and now legal option in many countries – pot? Or to stop yourself binge-eating, what if you binge-played video games instead?

10. Stop talking to your family

This is the most crucial resolution for the year ahead. Refrain from communicating with your family so that when the current polarising political situation blows over, you are still left with one. Once you have gone through your patient explanations of why the left side is better and not just while posing for a selfie, and in return, been inundated with memes calling you an 'intellectual terrorist', it is time to mute all family WhatsApp groups and your mouth as well. Else you may suffer the loss of property and propriety, as one friend discovered when her inebriated husband – who has taken to wearing his political allegiance not just on his sleeve but on his legs, in the form of bright-orange pants – slammed down his glass so hard in the midst of a heated argument that their side table cracked.

In case anyone is interested in my resolutions for the year, let me inform you that I didn't make any. Instead of wish lists, I tend to rely on weekly to-do lists. In the last few years, I have discovered that if I keep ticking off daily tasks, by the time 365 days have passed, I manage to fulfil resolutions that I didn't even know I had made in the first place.

18

HELLO MONA LISA, BYE JET SPRAY

Every fall, the monarch butterfly begins a 3,000 mile journey to Mexico. In spring, sandhill cranes converge in Nebraska. During summer, a large population of two-legged creatures clamber into metal tubes, change longitudes and latitudes, and check into hotel rooms that are often decorated in shades of brown. A soul-sucking palette that has only one advantage: It makes ketchup, crushed chips, sweat and semen encrusted on carpets and walls all turn invisible. We walk into bathrooms without jet sprays, stocked only with toilet paper.

We stack empty water bottles by the sink as a substitute for a lota, only to discover at critical moments that housekeeping has chucked them once again.

Armed with our cameras, we participate in these transient migrations for the same reasons we get married. It is based on the hope that by entering another state of being, or crossing-boundaries, we will instantly be fulfilled and satisfied. This seems to have no relevance to whether we were fulfilled and satisfied before entering the institution or the credit card–guaranteed room. The statistics for disappointing marriages and holidays are roughly the same. Despite this disconcerting fact, there are multiple reasons for depleting savings while jostling in crowded museums, trying to get a glimpse of Mona Lisa's enigmatic smile.

As the guards at the Louvre will tell you, even the most beautiful pieces of art turn invisible when you see them hanging around every day in the same place. Familiarity, contrary to the popular adage, does not breed contempt, merely indifference. Take the same painting, put it on another wall and we will appreciate the details again. Transport partners, children, friends to a different location and reclaim the ability to see the macramé patterns of relationships instead of just the holes.

If we are a summation of all that we remember, then travelling seems to create the strongest memories. The unknown and unusual takes us back to our primeval selves; sounds of a crunching twig indicating predator or prey. Senses engaged in the present create a gossamer web of neural impressions, binding the memory firmly in the centre.

My sharpest memory of eating a litchi is not at my dining table this summer, but on a swing in Jaipur over three decades ago. I remember the metal chains of the swing pushing into my back. My fingers poking into the top of the brick-red, bumpy skin till it parted, revealing the gelatinous, sweet flesh inside. The juice smeared across my mouth like I had applied lip gloss, the old roll-on ones that smelt of orange blossoms and astringent air fresheners. The pale flesh consumed till it revealed a glistening brown seed. I recall turning it around in my hand thinking it looked exactly like a cockroach bereft of antennae. And I remember Uncle, Manju Aunty's husband, though his first name is lost in the past, wearily trudging to the market once again because I had gobbled up the entire bushel of litchis he had bought that morning.

Sitting on a morning train, my head thudding against the window, I watch the man across me. Faded eyes and florid cheeks. Not the pink of youth but the one that comes with broken veins and time. I am curious about the wedding band on his middle finger. Widowed or weight loss? He gathers his coffee cup, the torn sugar sachet, creating a small, contained pile of garbage, picking up crumbs and dropping them into the cup. Widowed, I decide. A man used to cleaning up after himself. Ask me to describe what my accountant was wearing last week and I would be hard pressed for an answer.

To observe, we must be still. Paradoxically, it's easier to stay still when we are moving. Planes, trains, automobiles and rambling walks compel the mind to halt its endless skipping rope workout – three jumps in the future, two in the past – getting tangled up and tripping over repeatedly. Routine is commonly described as a fixed time to do fixed things. An elixir to enhance productivity, and a cage.

When we travel, devoid of routine, we wander, watch and wonder. We gaze at the grey river changing into a crinkled, embroidered navy with threads of glittering sequins. The swollen Buck Moon hanging low over the water, jeering the sun with its size. When did we last look at the moon in our own town, we ask each other, shaking our heads in disbelief.

We return altered and committed to holding onto the change. We must rediscover our own neighbourhood instead of taking the shortest route back home. Talk to the cobbler down the street, the way we asked the Maggi point vendor so many questions in Mussoorie. Have dinner with our partner across a candlelit table every week. Sprawl on a bench and look at the clouds, just like we did in the Jardin des Tuileries. We manage for a short period. Inevitably, we slip back into the straitjackets of structure.

Then we wait. To book tickets and clamber into metal tubes. Looking for the pieces of ourselves buried under the longitude and latitude of our lives.

If you keep turning and looking at the past, all you will get is a crick in your neck.

19

SITTING ON A GOLD MINE

9 a.m.: I am sitting on my balcony staring at the sea when my sister-in-law, who is also my sister-in-arms, decides to drop by before leaving for the gym. She asks me what I am doing, and when I tell her that I am performing a frantic though invisible task called thinking, she snorts, 'If you want to think so much, then think about this, is this house in your name?' I reply, 'What a funny question, it's our home, but I guess it's in your brother's name, so technically it's his, but how does it …'

And she interrupts triumphantly, 'But your jewellery is your own, right? Same pinch! That's why when the prime minister had announced that gold scheme a few years ago, I had been so excited. He said that women usually don't own anything. Houses and cars are in the name of their husbands or sons, but gold is a woman's strength and the gold scheme is to empower women. After I read that, I wanted to stand up and clap for him. I went straight to his website and I saw a notation, "Connect with the PM – Download App" and I clicked on it. With just a tap on my phone, I felt close to him, no matter which foreign country he was touring. He really is worth his weight in gold.' And with that, she totters off to spin class.

11 a.m.: Driving to the office, I spot a huge hoarding of Radhe Maa. Our prime minister must have seen one of these and thought that if he just gets her gold into circulation, then he could easily cut down on gold imports by a thousand tonnes or so.

2 p.m.: As I am deciding between broccoli and bhindi for dinner while checking a deck that we have to send out, my accountant walks in, 'Ma'am, some of our big clients are saying that since GST on candles is unlikely to change from 18 per cent in the upcoming reform, they want us to give them 15 per cent discount.'

'This GST is such a pain!' I moan.

'Yes Ma'am, the Good and Simple Tax is making business bad and life complicated.'

I reply, 'That's because GST doesn't stand for good and simple tax! It's goods and services tax. You should know this; you are an accountant, for God's sake!'

'Yes Ma'am, I also thought so, but right from the start only I heard many government people saying "good and simple tax", so I got confused.'

I say, 'They are all learning from our beloved prime minister, who is the master of all acronyms. He decided that RSVP doesn't stand for Répondez s'il vous plaît but for Rahul, Sonia, Vadra and Priyanka. Please tell our clients we are not offering any discounts at all!'

4.30 p.m.: Wanting to get my cousin a bangle for her birthday, I hop over to my jeweller. I find the perfect gift for her and also a few things for me. As the sales manager is getting my goodies packed, I ask her if she had seen any change in the buying habits of customers after government's gold scheme. She laughs, 'Madam, no lady is going to exchange her jewellery for bonds and certificates. I am not going to string the paper around my neck and wear it to a party na? I will proudly wear my navratna necklace so that Mrs Chadda, my proudy neighbour, will burn with jealousy and say, "Lovleen, such a beauty neckpiece, how much you got for?"'

The folks who decided that women will be the drivers of this gold bond scheme forgot that the main reason why most women buy gold is perhaps the same reason they once bought Onida TVs – 'Neighbour's envy, owner's pride'.

8 p.m.: The man of the house is chomping on Amritsari samosas while I am delicately sipping some green tea as I tell him about my day, 'The

intention to invest in bonds is great but I wish they would not try to put an amla on a cow-dung patty and call it a cherry cake by saying this is women's empowerment. Last Women's Day there were so many articles about how these gold bonds facilitate equality! To empower women, we have to radically change the attitude of men. If I joined politics, I would focus only on educating men about the role of women in society.'

The man of the house clears his throat and says, 'Mother India, then really, why don't you join politics?'

I look at him in horror, 'Have you seen what happens to all the people who join politics, it's terrifying!'

'What?' he asks.

'Haven't you noticed? Politicians and their weight gain!' I say, ' If I joined politics, I might, like most of them, start stuffing my face with countless samosas only to keep my mouth occupied so that it does not have the time to either scream or laugh out loud when fellow politicians spout their nonsense, like Mulayam Singh who said, "Should rape cases lead to hanging? Boys will be boys", or the Kerala education minister who once said that boys and girls should not sit together in class, or another benevolent CM advising aggrieved nurses not to protest in the sun because it will darken their complexion and thus hurt their marital prospects!'

The man of the house peers at me and says, 'Can I pause your moving speech to just tell you I got a notification about our credit card, so exactly what all did you buy at the jewellery store?'

Caught on the back foot, I quickly stuff a piece of samosa in my mouth and chew on the fact that, in some instances, silence is indeed golden.

If enough bricks are
thrown at you, you can
use them to build a house.

20

HOW THE LOVE CHARGER RAN OUT OF BATTERY

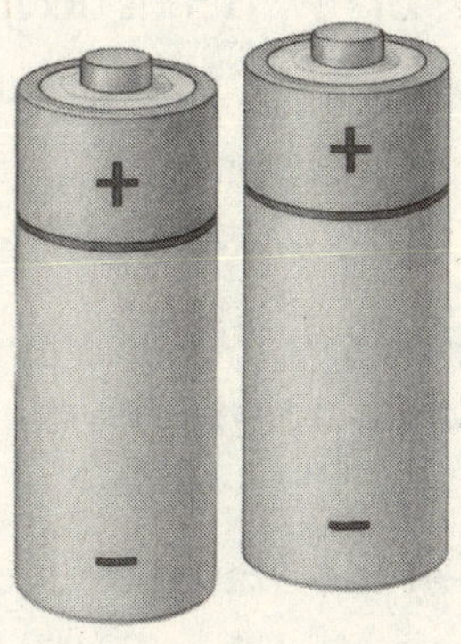

I seem to have an obsession with hairy godmen. I first realised this weakness when I became fixated on the hirsute Baba Ram Rahim Singh who also called himself MSG, an acronym for 'Messenger of God'. When the Baba decided to star in a movie, I began asking people to join my MSG club and come with me to catch the first day, first show of the good Baba's cinematic outing. I urged them to meet me at PVR Juhu wearing special T-shirts emblazoned with Ram Rahim's face, which you could buy online for 375 rupees.

Since I am no godman, conman or, for that matter, any sort of man at all, I got no applicants till, finally, three of my friends decided to help me save face and joined the MSG club.

To further amuse myself, I also regularly listened to MSG's songs with lyrics like, 'You are the Love Charger, billions battery when goes down, you charged up with love so strong.'

One day, I was at the Marriott when I discovered that Baba Gurmeet Ram Rahim Singh Insan had taken over the presidential suite, as well as dozens of rooms for a fortnight. I guess he probably needed the extra space even if it was to just store his mammoth name.

My Parsi assistant rather spitefully refused to let me linger in the lobby, waiting for a glimpse of my idol. But after I cursed her with 'I hope vultures eat you alive soon!', she grudgingly let me take a picture with MSG's lurid green convertible parked right outside.

A year later, while I was on my daily walk around the neighbourhood, I saw a convoy of cars and heavy police security. MSG had moved into my neighbourhood. I feverishly posted about my new neighbour along with pictures of garlanded bottles of Chinese seasoning. Soon enough, his top aide got hold of my number and, politely, asked me to shut the hell up.

It's not the first time I've been at the receiving end of a godman's wrath. I had once written a satirical column about a godwoman, and her friends in high places called up my mother, telling her that it would be safer for me to zip my lip. I had also been made to feel like a gigantic dartboard while observing a few connections between two godmen and their grouse with not getting the Nobel Prize, on X. Within hours of my post, I had been swarmed by their followers with threats that millions would boycott the man of the house's next film. But the realisation of what a godman's followers are really capable of sunk in only after MSG was convicted of rape. Mayhem spread across parts of Punjab and Haryana as his followers, who call themselves Insan, forgot about their humanity and promised to 'wipe out India'.

The violence led to at least thirty deaths and hundreds injured. The ministers, who had taken blessings from the same godman, looking at these very followers as a vote bank, could only claim helplessness.

There are times when I find myself pondering on pointless issues, like how much money these babas make off all their spiritual empires or how much time they must spend grooming their long hair and equally long beards. First, they probably need to oil, shampoo and condition both, with products that they are selling to the public at large. Then, of course, there are the monthly hair and beard dye jobs, unless their god-like powers also prevent them from greying, though most are past the fifty-year mark.

But ultimately, that is their business, both literally and figuratively speaking, and I am fine with it. What really bothers me is how we cut open our skulls and hand them our minds on a plate like the legendary delicacy, monkey brains.

When our current idol falls off his pedestal, we simply call him or her a fraud and go off on a quest to find the next one. It is time that we gullible fools stop turning towards them like a bunch of silly sunflowers looking for the sun, forgetting that a halo is just a trick of the light.

Anyway, since we have diverged to talking about tasty dishes, let me inform you that though years have passed since the Love Charger was arrested, my fascination with the topic has not ended, because even now when I go to Chinese restaurants, I tell the server, 'I don't want any monosodium glutamate in my Schezwan chicken anymore, you people should lock away your MSG too.'

21

REACHING THE TIPPING POINT WITH ADELE & MALALA

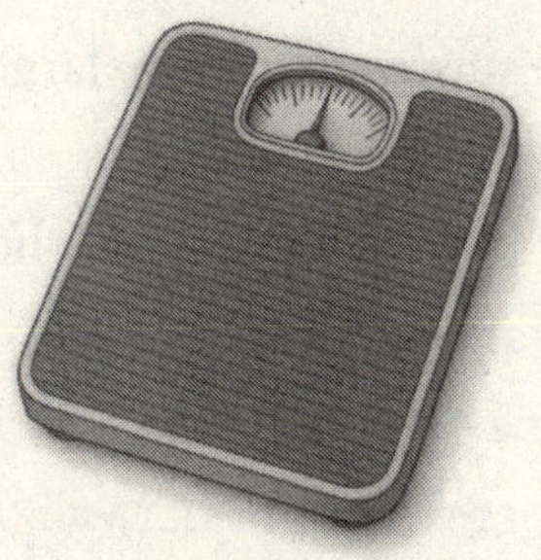

It's an anaconda of a voice. Jaws wide open, she draws you in. Octave by octave you surrender, cradled within a network of vocal cords. When you hear Adele performing 'Easy on Me', the phantom hairs on your arms stand, as if the follicles have forgotten they have all been lasered off.

When Adele made a comeback, the chatter had been more about her 100-pound weight loss than her album about heartbreak. There was a sense among her followers of being let down.

An assumption that by losing weight she had abandoned all the women who saw themselves visually represented through her.

'The most brutal conversations were being had by other women about my body,' she said in an interview. It makes you wonder why, with a voice that is so supremely extra-large, we are even talking about her dress size.

Women, though, live in a dichotomy where conditioning and aspirations come to a head repeatedly. I may tell you that Adele should not be defined by her weight or her weight loss, yet for the last twenty-four years, the weighing scale and I have had a daily conference where the numbers mock me and I get off and eat a cookie in despair.

Recently, I finally got rid of some stubborn pounds and I found myself showered with compliments including the ubiquitous, 'You have shrunk,' like I was a sweater that got accidentally thrown into the washing machine. These well-intentioned, banal statements did add a skip in my step, and I liked the way the dent in my sides could almost be mistaken for a defined waist.

There is a part of me that judges this as shallow, and so will a few who read this. There will also be a large section that will wonder, 'What diet did she go on, perhaps we should try it too.' Well, it was not keto, paleo, low cal or low fat. I got my weight-changing, and some life-changing, tips from an eighty-year-old. I had an opportunity to interview Waheeda Rehman, and she gave me some sagacious advice, 'Whenever I put on a kilo or so, I start eating omelettes for dinner till I lose it.' Since then, I have consumed so many omelettes that I have a feeling even my ovaries are now confused if the eggs floating around in my system are produced by them or an army of chickens.

Ageism, sexism, feminism and our own jism are all the weapons frequently used against us. While it's bad enough that we function within a patriarchal framework, it's odd that women often judge each other the most.

In a book on Uday Kotak, there is a snippet about how Nykaa founder Falguni Nayar, who recently became India's richest self-made woman billionaire with her successful IPO, wanted to quit her job and join her husband when she was being transferred to London and then New York. Instead, Uday Kotak asked her to stay on and start offices in those cities. Instead of applauding her business acumen, people are arguing about how she was doing a disservice to feminism by wanting to quit her job and follow her husband.

Marriages are not a public limited company where you are selling shares and need to give investors their money back. But they still seem to be everybody's businesses, instead of just yours. If I paid attention to the comments thrown my way, then either I should get a divorce because my partner and I hold opposing views on multiple issues or wear a sari and gyrate to 'Tip Tip Barsa Pani' on alternate weekends to keep the marriage alive.

On a dull afternoon, I decided to pay heed to the latter suggestion and make a video with my own rendition of the iconic song. Unfortunately, I ended up singing this to my plants with a watering can and not to the man everyone seems to serenade with it. This has less to do with not wanting to be objectified and more to do with my brain having an existential breakdown while doing hip rolls and singing off key. As I have explained in the video, I am just the sort of person who will start worrying about things like ...

1. Now I must send this sari to the laundry, can't just hang it back like all the ones I wear to wedding functions.
2. Shit! Water going into my ear will mean I can't hear the music, so how will I know when to sing and when to stop.
3. My period is meant to come the day after; I hope it's not planning on catching some early bird special to visit me right now.
4. How embarrassing if the children see me doing all this from the balcony.
5. Hanging out in wet clothes for so long, it's very likely I will get thrush or some other fungal infection!
6. My back is going to kill me. Better put some Iodex on it tonight.

7. And, of course, the most important part – no one is paying me for this!

Now that I have digressed enough to fall off a cliff, let me return to the tricky landscape of picking a life partner. As the world and especially all nosy buas know, Malala married Asser Malik. But besides blessings, Malala was also showered with terms like hypocrite and anti-feminist. All because in an earlier interview she had said, 'I still don't understand why people have to get married. If you want to have a person in your life … why can't it just be a partnership?' Meanwhile, I am left wondering, if you take a bullet to the head for standing up for other girls, the least you could be allowed to do is change your mind?

In my opinion, Malala must join Adele in crooning, 'I was still a child. Didn't get the chance to feel the world around me. Had no time to choose. What I chose to do. So go easy on me.'

It doesn't matter if you are an icon like these women or the only people following you are the twenty-two members of your extended family on Instagram, you will all be judged. If you are single, you better get married. Married, then where are the children? Working women, aren't you neglecting the kids? If you don't work, then you are setting a bad example for the same brats. Do you agree with your husband? You are such a doormat! And if you disagree, then why are you still with him? Those lines on your forehead make you look like a dadi amma! Are you using Botox to wipe off the wrinkles? How fake! And if, like Malala, you change your mind, which should be a natural progression of growing older and hopefully wiser, then you are clearly a fraud.

It's almost comical that no matter what you choose to do, there will always be people telling you that your choices are not good enough. Tragically, after hearing it time and again, we begin to believe all these voices too. So, how about, for a change, we listen to Adele and go easy on each other and especially on ourselves.

22

WHEN LOVE FLIES OUT OF THE TRAIN WINDOW

In the early days – when love is still blind but has yet to turn deaf, when tarnished memories are pulled out and polished brightly by the gleam of interest in one's partner's eyes, when there are layers slowly revealed and some firmly hidden – we, like most new couples, exchanged myriad stories.

One evening, I told him about a train ride that ended my romance with the railways. In 1989, I decided to get a job as an interior designer's assistant. Feeling independent and rather grown up, I would take the train to Charni Road Station every day. During the scramble of rush hour, I would push my way in, while a horde of women simultaneously got off. On one such occasion, as I clambered onto the train, the shoulder strap of my purse got entangled around a slender, sari-clad disembarking passenger's neck while I was left holding on to the bottom bit for dear life. The train started moving and she had to run alongside, as the purse strap had now become a noose around her neck. 'I was in a terrible dilemma,' I told him. 'If I held on to my purse, she could get strangled or pulled under the train and if I let go, I would be on the train with no money, no ID and no handy mobile phone in the back pocket as mobiles didn't even exist!'

'So what did you do?' he asked, and I replied, 'Since I am not in a cell for homicidal maniacs, you can probably guess what I did! I let go and lost both my bag and my love for train journeys.'

Sitting beside me on our terrace that cloudy night, he, in turn, told me his tale, set against the cadences of a chugging railway engine.

'Starting from the seventh standard, every morning, I would take the Harbour line to get to my school, Don Bosco.'

He then drew a vivid picture of a rainy August day, where he walked towards the compartment exit, standing behind a woman with an incongruously long plait, who also disembarked at his stop, King's Circle Station. 'Over time,' he explained, 'You start recognising faces; the usual suspects crammed into the same compartment on their way to their daily grinds.'

Another familiar face, a tall man with a well-groomed moustache rushed across the compartment, making his way towards them with an umbrella in his hand. He hesitantly addressed the woman, 'I think you forgot your umbrella!' She thanked him profusely. Leaving her umbrella behind would have meant getting drenched in the rain, as well as having to purchase another one.

'Though I usually spent my time reading Phantom comics on the train, I began noticing that the woman with the long plait and the man who handed her the umbrella had started smiling at each other from the far ends of the compartment.'

Time went by and they were soon sitting together, cocooned in whispered conversations and joyful laughter. A few months later, she started carrying snacks for them to share before she got off at her stop. He paused for a long moment, and I recall impatiently asking him, 'Then what happened?'

He said, 'The best thing! Summer holidays began!'

'That's your story? That's the end?'

He shook his head, 'No! But perhaps it should have been.'

The school holidays lasted a glorious two months, but then it was time to board the train back to Don Bosco. He saw the pair sitting together in the compartment again. She now had a mangalsutra around her neck while he sported a tender smile, as she rested her head on his shoulder.

'Time marched on; I was in tenth standard now. Bruce Lee was my new hero, and I started learning martial arts. I used to spend the dreary commute daydreaming, my mind filled with scenes from *Enter the Dragon* and *Fist of Fury*.'

The twosome on the train were also engrossed in their respective worlds. The wife, her hair now wound in a bun, kept herself busy with a ball of yellow yarn and a pair of knitting needles, while her husband seemed content to nap. And then came a day of torrential rainfall with the familiar lament of flooded roads and delayed commutes.

'The next stop was King's Circle Station. The woman moved towards the exit. I was standing right behind her when her husband brusquely called out to her, "And this? Who is going to pick this up, your naukar?" Her eyes downcast, she silently brushed past me, retraced her steps and picked up her black umbrella.'

German philosopher Erich Fromm said that love is an art, just as living is an art; if we want to learn how to love, we must proceed in the same way like we want to learn any other art, say music or painting. But most of us see love as an acquisition rather than an art, like a new phone that we gaze at reverently as we take it out from the box and gently cradle in our hands.

The first time it falls, there is an anguished gasp. We snatch it up from the ground, meticulously examine it for small scuffs, and carefully put it back in our pockets. Soon, we begin tossing it around nonchalantly, unperturbed by the falls and tumbles. One fine day, we look at the scratches and dents, and murmur to ourselves, 'Perhaps it's time to get a new one again.'

Marriage may not be a bed of roses. Which is a bit of a relief – otherwise you would be constantly pricked as you lay there, rather than just twice a week and when the kids are fast asleep.

23

MOTHER EMERITUS

Having a child is similar to undergoing a lobotomy. Before an army of mothers attacks me with soiled diapers, let me make it clear that this statement is backed by scientific research. Women's brains scanned during and after pregnancy showed significant changes. Researchers believe that these alterations make a mother prioritise her child's demands over all other tasks. It basically compels her to stop being the Sherlock Holmes of her own story and go straight to playing Mrs Hudson, the landlady of Holmes's Baker Street flat.

Technically, these changes should revert once the baby doesn't require immersive care, but the brain is a creature of habit. This revelation struck me right after a phone call with our health insurance agent in the UK. The wheezy man was explaining why my premiums were increasing this year, and being part Gujarati, this was causing me physical distress. Wondering if I should move to a cheaper plan with fewer allocated GP visits, I asked him, 'Can you tell me how often my two dependents on the plan have used their allotted visits?'

In a stilted British accent, he stated he could give me my daughter's information but not my son's. 'He is not a minor, so he would have to give you access to this information. We can't compromise his privacy.'

The Indian mother in me was immediately offended. Does this White man not know that there is no such thing as privacy in our households? We tell people it's called a joint family to make it sound palatable. Technically it should be called a conjoined family – with one head, a dozen chattering mouths and multiple limbs, all stitched up together.

I protested, 'But he is my son! All his organs that come under your policy have been created by me.' But the agent stuck to his stance.

When I messaged the prodigal son for access to his account, I received a curt reply. 'Mom, I have made only four visits in the entire year, and you know that because you insisted on coming with me for all of them! While I am happy to answer all your questions, I am not giving you my password. I am twenty-two, not twelve; I can handle it.'

He has been pushing back for a while, but this year, the boundaries seem to have grown from chalk lines on the ground to looming electric fences.

Cleaning up his room that afternoon, I came across a box with 'Important Things' scribbled on the lid in a red marker pen. Inside, he had stored some childhood treasures. A molar that the tooth fairy, or rather I, must have forgotten to collect, pictures with his friends, a card from his dad and a letter I had written to him on his thirteenth birthday.

The day had started on a disastrous note because his name had been misspelt on the cake. It had 'Happy Birthday Aarve' written on it instead of 'Happy Birthday Aarav'. I had tried fobbing him off by saying that the pastry chef was secretly a member of the Shiv Sena and changed it because he thought Aarve sounds better than Aarav just like Mumbai sounds better than Bombay but he did not believe me. I had then written him this long letter to make up.

Dear son,

I don't know why a certain age is specified as a step into your teens or what that even really means, except that you are sprouting hair in odd places and sprouting even odder ideas. But the fact remains that this is your big thirteenth birthday, so here is a letter from dear Mom that you may lose, as you have lost so many of my notes in the past.

I thought you were just careless till I realised that you still have the autographed picture of Superwoman, so I guess you just misplace those objects that you know I can help you find again.

With every year that goes by, I have to loosen these strings that tie me to you because you are untying the knots at such great speed at your end that if I don't let go, then all that rope will just tangle around me and I won't find a way out of this particular maze.

Thirteen years you have been as much my teacher as I have been yours. I learnt optimism, kindness and wonder from you as I taught you math, a few manners and how to switch the lights off when you leave the room.

But looking at you growing up and listening to you repeatedly tell me how much you are looking forward to your independence, I have started realising that when you finally leave my home, my world, and step into your own, my lights will go off automatically and my world will be filled with a bleak darkness. Though whenever you return for a visit, I will light numerous diyas and pretend that this is not a permanent power failure; we are just celebrating Diwali.

Some of this you will not understand till perhaps you have a child of your own but keep this letter as safe as that picture of Superwoman just in case, years from now, you forget how much you meant to me. For if you misplace this piece of information, I may not always be there to help you find it again.

Love you forever,

Your Mother

I clearly recall the man of the house teasing me when I had shown him the draft on my iPad and saying, 'So when you write this out properly on paper, are you going to use a pen or, to match the melodrama, do you want to use my blood and a chopstick?'

The prodigal son, unlike his father, clearly valued my words. I was touched he had saved my letter and it made me miss the little boy he had once been even more.

That evening, the man of the house was glued to some game where a bunch of men chase one ball to prove that they have two each. Sitting beside him complaining about the prodigal son, I noted that businessmen, including our seventy-hour work week advocating Narayana Murthy, take on the honorary title 'chairman emeritus' when they retire.

'Perhaps I should also retire from this motherhood business and just keep an honorary title. "Mother emeritus" does have a nice ring to it,' I said.

The man of the house replied, 'Why are you moaning about an empty nest when our daughter is still here, and you seem to always be busy working anyway? And what does this emeritus-demeritus mean, can't you just use normal words instead of being a maha pakau all the time?'

It was no point telling him that it didn't matter that I have a company to run, a book to finish, columns to write and a younger child's hair to detangle. Mothering my eldest had been such a big part of my life that now that he didn't need me, I felt completely useless. Even my diary had maudlin entries like: 'A mother is like a pack of cold cuts with an expiry date stamped across it. After that period, you are simply forgotten at the back of the fridge till someday you rot and have to be discarded.'

Remember that neural rewiring we discussed at the beginning? Those pathways were clearly having an existential crisis. While there are hundreds of books on how to deal with babies, toddlers and teenagers, there are very few resources on how to continue being a mother when your child has left his childhood in the rear-view mirror. I decided to tap into someone who has had almost fifty years of experience in the business – my mother.

Over dinner, eating the parwal that she had insisted on heaping onto my plate, I said, 'Mom, my job is to take a bullet for my child. Why do you think I spent all those years practising by giving your grandson a nerf gun and standing within range? And now I have no say in anything he does! When I give him advice, he says I am nagging!'

'But you do the same thing,' she said. 'Every time I tell you about your hair, or try to fix it just before we are stepping onto the red carpet, you push my hand away and say you can do it yourself, so why are you complaining now? And weren't you the one who once told me that unsolicited advice is just interference? Good, that you are getting a taste of your own medicine.'

Disgruntled but trying to look at the bright side, I had to concede that humble pie does taste better than parwal and is also calorie-free. But this talk with Mom gave me a clue on how to approach the problem. I didn't have to put myself in my son's shoes to understand the situation. I just had to make a list of all the ways I feel my mother tries to coddle me and ensure that I stop doing the same to him. Number one being not fidgeting with his hair. And the unsolicited advice-interference part is true. We don't go around randomly telling our friends that they need to take vitamin D, then go buy it for them, insist they have it in front of us and check their mouths to make sure they have swallowed it. But we often do things like these to our children even when they are closer to middle-age than to puberty.

Our adult children do not need other adults hovering around them. They need supportive friends, and if we want to continue being a part of their lives, then we should assume that position or, like the Chinese, write petitions to make offspring visits a constitutional right.

Though I have an undeniable compulsion to hold on to my children, it would be wise to remember that they are like the air stored in my lungs, in my custody for just a moment before the next exhalation. This may not be an entirely correct analogy because unlike breaths we can't keep popping babies in and out constantly. I suppose we are more like garden hoses. A hosepipe's job is not to mourn the absence of ejected water, but to guide it in the right trajectory.

24

FATHER'S DAY, FOR ME, WILL ALWAYS BE IN DECEMBER

If my father hoped for a boy as his firstborn, I was never told. All I know is what he said to my mother – that I was the best present she could have ever given him as I entered the world, feet first, on his thirty-first birthday.

He always called me Tina Baba, never baby, and though I didn't realise it at that point, my upbringing was different from all the other young girls around me. The restrictions drawn around their adolescence did not define mine. The permanent marker, one that would later be passed onto their husbands, to enforce the circle of captivity did not exist in my case.

He was the one who gave me my first sip of alcohol, Scotch on the rocks, in a glass too heavy for my hand. I was permitted to peer into the living room with its shaggy white carpet and its bejewelled people. The light from the chandelier was diffused by the smoke that enveloped the room like a diaphanous veil, then the epitome of liberated sophistication. Dunhill, it said on the strewn cartons, the colour of congealing blood, their value further enhanced, because like the chocolates and the biscuits, it was all 'imported'. Cancer was not in our lexicon then, let alone emblazoned on the packets to dampen their beguilement.

There was an assortment of people that drifted in and out of my house and my life. Nothing was shielded and everything explained, one way or the other.

I got tips on how to improve my eyesight from a choreographer's mistress, a wiry middle-aged woman with burnished wavy hair and long-sleeved blouses, her failed attempts at suicide covered by floral handkerchiefs tied around her wrists. I stole cheese from platters meant for renowned musicians as they hummed their new compositions. A legion of writers, filmmakers and artists would saunter in and out, all part of his nightly durbars.

He always had time for us, though. Each night he would come to our bedroom, wearing a striped nightshirt with 'I love San Francisco' embroidered over the front pocket. 'Good night, sweet dreams, love you, miss you,' he would say. My sister and I would repeat the same. A nightly ritual that never changed, not the words or the sequence in which they were said.

Our summers were spent in Kashmir, and I can't recall what we did in the winters, but I do remember our birthdays. I would sit on the stairs; the December air sometimes cool enough to wear a sweater and watch the trucks filled with flowers entering the gate. They were, of course, for him, but all of eight, I thought they were for my birthday.

The '70s were a time when fathers were bystanders in the pursuit of parenting. A dad was merely someone who stood in the wings, passing props – Hula Hoops and gleaming crowns – to the characters rushing on and off the stage, including the person in the main lead, the mother. My father was the same. He didn't help with homework or pack my snack dabba. Though, unlike other parents, he always spoke to me like an equal.

When I started dating, we exchanged advice. He told me that he was looking for a partner who would lie down in his lap so they would read the same book together.

I laughed, 'Dad, this is never going to happen. Your expectations are ridiculous. What if they read slower than you or want to take a break? Just find a decent woman who can tolerate your nonsense and that should be enough.'

He was equally sagacious with me. 'Don't have one boyfriend,' he once said to me. 'Always have four at a time, that way your heart will never be broken.'

A suggestion that held me in good stead, though I never told him that he was the only man who had the power to break my heart.

A daughter needs her father's presence in her life for many reasons. What she needs most is to know that she has someone to lean on, to depend upon, besides herself. My father may not have been standing by my side, holding my hand through every stage of life, but somewhere deep inside, I knew that I could count on him. When he looked at me, regardless of how angry he was, there was a singular reflection, one that never faltered – his complete belief in me. He may have accused me on multiple occasions of being 'over-smart' but never once did he make me feel dumb.

He was a brilliant man, bright, articulate but not particularly easy to deal with. We argued over innumerable things. I had inherited his rosy cheeks, his crinkling eyes, his weak ankles and his fiery temper. We were both readers, and though I could discuss Shakespeare with him, I was never sure if he was the King Lear to my Cordelia or the Atticus Finch to my Scout.

In the end, it didn't matter. Nothing did. A laundry list of complaints on two sides of the same page, washed away by the most brutal of all erasers – death.

It was only after he was gone that I heard from all his friends how he would show them my poetry. He would tell them that I would be a writer someday. He said I was his favourite, his son. For a man of that generation, where gender was not a social construct but an entire identity, a son meant someone capable, someone worthy of being relied upon perhaps in his mind. There could not have been a finer compliment.

Loss is not a constant ache, nor does it come equipped with a full stop. It lives between pauses and emerges at unexpected moments. Sometimes it's a song on the radio or when I am applying kohl and I see his eyes, under the same arched brows staring out of my reflection. It is lurking within every birthday when I wake up in excitement before my heart sinks. The man who loved words, always used them in a precise order. These things could not be tampered with, replaced or changed. Just the way he didn't like anyone moving his books, glasses and packets of Dunhill.

Year after year, he said the same thing. Something that no one else can ever say again, 'Happy birthday to you too, Tina Baba.'

Father's Day may fall in June, but for me, it will always be in December.

25

WHAT ANIMALS CAN TEACH US ABOUT LUV, SHUV AND SHAADI

Amid a backdrop of icy-grey acacia trees, four elephants stood in a trance. A female, recognisable by the geometric planes of her head, and three bull elephants. Perched on the bouncing seats of a khaki jeep, I had stumbled upon a primeval mating ritual. The elephants moved slowly. Approaches. Rejections. Swiping right and left with their trunks.

The mating was short-lived and clumsy. Like a section of Indian men, bull elephants also seem to believe that if two minutes are good enough for Maggi noodles, then it's good enough for them. Our safari guide, who could be mistaken for Shikari Shambu, informed us that the elephants would mate several times over the next few days and then go their own way. The resulting calf would be raised by a herd of predominantly female elephants.

This was a common phenomenon among the mammals I spotted in Tanzania: lionesses protecting their cubs and tiny wildebeests running alongside their moms and aunts. Communities of females raising their young, with males either absent or wandering in and out without doing much of the heavy lifting.

I found it intriguing how we humans evolved from these collective structures into units of two and decided that our mating rituals had to include both monogamy and matrimony. Why did we confine ourselves in a 2BHK, hum-do-hamare-do cage? And if marriage is about everlasting love, why does it seem to run out faster than an Eveready battery?

A little digging into history brought up a startling fact. The concept of marriage had initially nothing to do with love but was due to the advent of agriculture. When we were nomads, it didn't matter if the child you were carrying was Sharma ji's from the neighbouring cave or that foolish Desai's who was scared of the rain. Then came farming, and land became an ownable commodity. Men needed to ensure that only their biological children would inherit their assets. Enter wedlock, a mechanism to tie down a woman by making the prosperity of her children dependent on her monogamy. Only around the eighteenth century did luv, shuv and all that entailed enter the fray.

While a marriage does have its chafing issues, it has some surprising medical advantages. A recent paper published in the *Annals of Behavioural Medicine* found that people who never married were twice as likely to die early as those in solid marriages. It's men, though, who seem to wither away without partners, while women tend to put on their lipstick and just get on with it. There is also enough research that shows raising a family with a reliable partner has definite advantages over being a single parent. But how do you sleep next to a partner when, at least twice a week, you are overcome with the urge to strangle them – and that's not counting the times when their snoring is louder than the baboons chattering outside your tent. While philosophers and self-help gurus dissect human nature, I chose to focus on nature itself, observing the techniques animals use as their survival often hinges on a delicate balance of cooperative hunting strategies and symbiotic relationships.

1. Hyena's Hustle: Hyenas don't battle with lions for a share of the kill. They approach stealthily and run away with a juicy bit. Instead of constant confrontations, perhaps sometimes we should just resort to trickery. When your partner starts singing Punjabi songs at ear-shattering decibels, asking him to stop may become a battle of freedom like

he is Gandhi ji fighting for swaraj. Instead, distract him with questions like, 'What was that movie we saw that day with that guy? It was on Netflix, remember?' While his mind does multiple cartwheels, enjoy the blissful silence.

2. Bonhomie of Baboons: I watched baboons grooming each other and playing together. These creatures tend to live in large groups where females make lifelong bonds. After entering a relationship, women especially tend to concentrate primarily on their partners. Focus is a dangerous thing if directed only in one direction. It's how a magnifying glass sets paper on fire. Perhaps we are better off strengthening our social network like baboons. Basically, keep your man close but your girlfriends even closer.

3. Giraffe's Gaze: Giraffes seem to be eternally scanning the landscape. In relationships as well, it's better to look through a wide-angle

instead of a zoom lens. Your partner's poor jokes and preference for mummy's rajma can feel like significant grievances in the moment but fade away a week later.

4. Hint from Hippos: Hippos communicate through grunts, roars and sprays of water. Our guide told us that these signals convey their moods and avoid conflicts within their group. Communication in a marriage is often not about what you are saying but how you present it. I have a friend who, whether she is asking her husband to empty the bin or share her biryani, always begins by calling him 'Baby'. I used to laugh at her in our twenties, but looking at them still going strong three decades later, I have to say that effective communication is the true Fevicol ka Jod.

5. Cheetah's Composure: Cheetahs are gifted with speed, but they wait and go for the kill only when the time is right. Instead of getting into heated discussions over whose turn it

was to take your kid shopping for sneakers and why dirty clothes are on the floor, wait till you both have downed a glass of wine or whatever beverage helps you see the world through rose-tinted glasses. Then, when your partner, like the grazing impala, has his guard down, launch your attack.

On our last game drive, we saw another herd, with a solitary bull elephant walking far ahead of the females with calves. The bull elephant had my husband's sympathies. 'Poor guy, he is all alone.' I was more focused on how the male could wander off as he pleased, while the females had to take care of the young. That, I suppose, is marriage in a nutshell – two people looking at the same scenario with different interpretations and then bickering over right and wrong.

Driving back to camp that evening, the guide pointed out a pair of birds called tik-tik who are so devoted to each other that when one dies, the other sometimes kills itself by eating poisonous grass. I told my husband, 'Acha, if I die first, you better eat poisonous grass too. If I see your second wife walking around with my handbags, I promise I will come and haunt you both.'

He shook his head and replied, 'I want to eat that poisonous grass right now, at least then I won't have to listen to all this nonsense.' Then he swatted a mosquito on my arm, the human equivalent of baboons delousing each other. We continued engaging in the complex choreography of cooperation, affection and mutual tolerance as our jeep raced against the setting sun.

Rakhi is a big affair at my in-laws' and we usually have a theme party to make it even more exciting. This year it was meant to be a 'Chinese party'.

When I protested about cultural appropriation, Mummy ji was alarmed.

'No, no, we are not doing any operation, just wearing fancy dress.'

I explained what the word meant, and she replied, 'If that is a problem, then people should stop ordering Chinese food also. It is all give and take, Beta, this your culture, my culture thing. Anyway, we have given the Chinese more than they have given us. Think about it, we gave them Buddhism, and in return, we got veg manchurian!'

26

TIME TO GIN AND BEAR IT, BABUMOSHAI

At the start of my fiftieth year on this watery planet, I grew weary of women my age talking about ageing gracefully. 'Grace counts in ballet, and ageing is a battle! But … thanks to the ageing process, I can't quite remember if I read this somewhere or made it up just now,' I told a friend who, along with emptying her bank account while replenishing her dermatologist's, was busy equating grace with being frozen in time, starting with her forehead.

I felt I had finally reached the mid-point between growing and slowly dying. This could be likened to balancing on top of a bell jar. Having clambered up one side, the only thing left to do was slide down the other, either with a sudden crunch, or a slow glide accompanied by an orchestra of creaking joints and leaking valves.

This epiphany didn't arrive with a bang. Instead, it was ensconced in a bubble of calm. This summer, on the family WhatsApp chat, I boasted, 'It is true that you get wiser as you get older. I have stopped getting annoyed and seem to have a lot more patience. Or perhaps it's all the yoga. It's finally kicked in because I almost feel like a yogi now.'

My iridescent bubble popped as soon as I had a routine blood test that stated my testosterone had plummeted to zero. The side effect of this perimenopausal fluctuation was a lack of aggression along with lethargy. In other words, I had hormonally acquired the ability to sit in one place and do nothing – not that different from a yogi after all.

This news hit me harder than finding grey hair in my eyebrow. For a large part of my life, I had been energetically coasting on such high levels of testosterone that in the '90s, when woke was just the opposite of sleep, I used to make jokes like, 'I am more of a man than most men I meet, and with the balls as well.' Now, I was left with low energy and a few stale jokes.

There were other distinct disadvantages to this getting older business. Like the bluethroat birds who migrate from Alaska to Rajasthan in winter, it really starts going all south after a certain age. Hair shifts from your head and appears on your chin. The fat from the cheeks sinks to form squishy jowls. Breasts start reaching out to embrace your knees.

Not wanting to face reality and, thanks to my worsening eyesight, not having to see it in the mirror as well, I tried ignoring the fact that my 'big birthday' was around the corner. When that didn't work, I began pre-empting it by telling people I was fifty. On one occasion, my younger one corrected me, 'No Mama, you are still forty-nine.'

Taking a sip of my drink, because why grin and bear it when you can use gin and bear it, I told her, 'This about-to-turn-fifty business is like a railway journey, even if it's to Ulhasnagar and not a destination you particularly want to reach, you still want to just get there and get off the train.'

I was clearly having an existential crisis because I sat with a calculator one evening and created a rough timeline. If I lived to a decent eighty-five, I had to first minus the fifty years that I had already spent. Then I had to multiply eight hours a day into 365 days into the approximate thirty-five years left, because that's the time I would spend sleeping, and then minus that sum from my timeline, which left me with a mere twenty-four years of living ahead. I only felt better when I recalled a famous dialogue recited by someone whose eyes crinkled just like mine: 'Babumoshai, zindagi badi honi chahiye, lambi nahi.'

It took a few months, but I began realising that this sliding down the bell jar, swift or slow, wouldn't be much fun if I kept moaning about it. Perhaps it is tougher for women to age because of the value placed on our appearance. Men, or at least most Indian men, start off life looking like the back of a dented bus and continue in that manner, just gathering a few more dents. Their self-esteem and power aren't contained within tight skin and pouty lips.

Leaving this superficial war fortified by marketing campaigns and evolutionary cues, I decided to list other advantages of ageing. I started with the fact that I was not freezing in the London winter because my hot flashes seemed more efficient than any Marks and Spencer thermal vest. Crossing middle age also meant that I was past the stage where you tend to know a little about everything but not enough about anything, including yourself. It is also a time when you have given up worrying about love, are yet to worry about health, and even work has stopped giving you sleepless nights.

The next chronological stop, though, seemed more daunting. I had started discovering that ageing works like Mr India's watch. One minute you are visible and the next, you disappear. As your eyesight worsens, it's other people who have problems seeing you and when you start using a hearing aid, they are the ones who turn a deaf ear to what you say. Hitting my sixties and seventies, I suppose the greatest benefit will be achieving liberation from societal norms. No one can tell you what to do: Young people don't notice you, people your age are just trying to find a sitting position that does not ache, and the older people who have always told you what to do are now all dead.

It may be time to appreciate that each stage of life is different. As a teenager, the notion of time was like looking up at the night sky – vast, infinite, twinkling with distant possibilities. Now it was like a boiled sweet stuck inside a cheek, the one you keep poking with your tongue as it shrinks in size. Or a chewing gum that is losing flavour, or a half-eaten lychee that is more seed than flesh. I am also starting to realise that all my metaphors are about food because who knows when it will end up replacing sex as the primary source of pleasure.

More than the actual ageing process, I suspect we are scared by the prospect of it. It reminds me of getting ready to swim, hesitating on the dock while anticipating the chill of the river water. Till you jump in, startled by the splash, water going into the nose. Then with a few kicks and strokes, you get accustomed to the temperature. Ageing, I have slowly come to believe, is only a battle if you try to fight the current.

A NOTE ON THE AUTHOR

Twinkle Khanna is one of India's bestselling authors and most widely read columnists. Her first book, *Mrs Funnybones*, was based on her newspaper columns. She went on to publish *The Legend of Lakshmi Prasad*, a collection of feminist short stories, the novel *Pyjamas Are Forgiving*, and most recently *Welcome to Paradise*, a critically acclaimed collection of stories. She has a master's degree in fiction writing from Goldsmiths, University of London.